Christm

Mehtas

MALIKA GANDHI

To Shital,
Hope You enjoy the book,

With love,

M. Gandhi ♡ ☺
— feb 2021 —

ACKNOWLEDGEMENTS AND THANKS

My sincere thanks to my editor, Victoria Froud from Positive Points Editorial Services, for helping me in getting this book out. I thank her for her profound enthusiasm, and the time she has dedicated to me and my book.

In addition, I thank my family, who supported me the writing of this book, especially on those days when I refused to write!

CONTENTS

Chapter One

A blizzard was on its way. That's what the weatherman said and this time, he was right. Rianna watched the snow falling on the pavement from inside her shop window and shivered, even though the central heating was on. Flakes swirled in a hurry to touch base, causing disruption to the Christmas shoppers.

It was almost 5pm, and Clara, Rianna's friend and assistant, had just finished putting up the Christmas décor. The lights on the tree twinkled and reflected off the bright silver baubles, making the whole thing come alive. The shop window sparkled with fairy lights, and the bookshelves were bright with Christmas cheer.

Naturally, her mother hated that she owned a bookshop.

"Why can't you be a lawyer, an accountant, a doctor? That's what a Gujarati does. They don't open up bookshops!" her mother, Lata, said.

"But it is a business," her dad, Rajni, approved. "And we Gujarati's do business, right?"

Rianna loved her dad; he always took her side.

It had always been Rianna's dream to own a bookshop, and when she turned twenty, she asked her dad for a loan. Luckily for her, her family were rich and so her dad gifted her the money.

"There is no need to pay me back, *beta*. I trust you one hundred percent. You know what you are doing."

Rianna knew how her shop would look and she wasted no time in setting it up when she had signed the lease contract and she had the keys. The shop was large and seemed stark and clinical when she first saw it, but she soon made it cosy.

Bookshelves lined the sides of the shop, with some lone standing ones in the middle. It was sort of a maze with comfy colourful sofas dotted around. Rianna made sure there was a cute children's section where the little ones could read and play with puppets and toys. This brought in the parents, and they always left with purchases.

Her parents owned an Indian sweet shop. Everyone loved their sweets, like the *ladwas*, the *barfis*, the *gulab jamboos*, and then there were their savoury foods such as the *ghatiyas*, the *sevs*, and the *chevdas*.

Her mouth watered just thinking about it. But most of all her father was a businessman, he understood money and money understood him. He advised her to put in a coffee shop.

"It will draw the customers in," he said. He was right.

It wasn't always about business though. They made time for family, Diwali being the main event, when the whole family that included both her father and mother's sides, getting together. Like every other year, this year was fabulous once again. It was her city, Leicester, that made it even more special.

The community would come together and celebrate Diwali on the Golden Mile, a road where every Indian sweet shop, sari and lehenga shop, and every Indian restaurant was open for the tourists and the locals. It was where the Diwali lights came on and when Sabras radio boomed out their Bollywood music.

But now it was December and Christmas day wasn't far, and she was ready to celebrate again. There was something about this time of year that made her feel engulfed with warmth. She looked forward to everything about Christmas, like the tree, the décor, the food and drink, and the parties with her friends.

"You did a brilliant job, Clara," Rianna praised, looking around at the decorations.

"It looks good, doesn't it? But I still think the tree needs colour," Clara said.

"You know, I like the simplicity."

"Wow, it's coming down fast out there." Clara meandered to the window where Rianna stood. "I hope it stops soon. Why can't the snow be big and fluffy, like cotton wool falling out of the sky?" Clara turned her back to the snow and began arranging a pile of new Christmas books on the Christmas table at the front.

"Hmm, good question. Let's ask the weatherman, shall we?"

"Ha ha, very funny. Listen, what are you doing on Christmas day?"

Christmas day. That was going to be interesting but exciting at the same time. Her uncle, her father's older brother, owned a cottage by a lake in the Lake District. He lived in Windermere and asked if they, the Mehtas, could look after it for him on Christmas day, as *you usually don't do anything.* The nerve!

"You see, we are flying to New York for the Christmas holiday. I'm sure you will understand," her uncle, Sailesh, said.

Uncle Sailesh was filthy rich. He owned a few holiday homes in Windermere and Scotland. He had plans to buy some homes in Wales and Northern Ireland, too.

Rajni contemplated the idea.

"You can use the house as you want, you know, I don't mind. Enjoy the countryside and lake this Christmas. Relax, brother."

"Well, it looks like I have to accept."

"Good, good!" Uncle Sailesh clicked off the landline. Everyone had mobile phones now. It infuriated Rianna that her father and uncle refused them.

"We are going to the Lake District this year," said Rianna, coming back to the present. "My uncle owns a cottage there. I've heard it's magical at this time of the year."

"And bloody cold, too," said Clara with a shiver of her own.

"And I hope, magical. So, what are you doing?"

"Nothing much. It's just me and mum. Dad buggered off with his young girlfriend, who is my age. Did I tell you that? Still can't get over it. And my brother is away in Paris. Lucky bugger. He is taking his long-term girlfriend. I bet he will propose to her. Some people have all the luck."

"Then make the most of the day with your mum; make it special." Rianna wished she could say more to console her friend, but what more could she have done?

"I have a question, seeing as we are talking about families."

"Go on."

"I've been wondering, and I think it is time you moved out. I mean you are 25 and you are an independent businesswoman, you know, I think it's time."

"Not that again!" Rianna rolled her eyes but she was amused. "I've told you before, that's not how it works in Indian families. We live with our parents until we are married. We move away for reasons such as work, or as I have heard, people of our age are now buying homes as an investment. But anyway, *I* wouldn't move out. I'd miss my mum's cooking too much; I'd miss my dad and my little sister."

The bell above the door rang as two customers walked in, the last remnants of the snow melting away on their coats.

"So glad you are still open, dear," said the old woman. "Half the shops have closed already, and we had nowhere to shelter. That storm is horrendous! I saw your shop and I couldn't resist some hot tea and a scone. You are still open, aren't you?" Hope twinkled in the woman's eyes. Rianna was about to close, but…

"I'll get you one right away," Rianna smiled.

The couple left with smiles after purchasing of some books. Rianna bade them goodbye and proceeded to shut shop and clean up with Clara.

Rianna gave Clara a lift home as usual. They both lived in Humberstone so it wasn't out of her way. It hardly ever snowed in her city but this year, it looked like things were going to be different. She hoped it snowed on Christmas Day where she was going. That would be magical!

Her mother opened the door as she got out of her Yaris.

"Quickly, get in before you get wet! I'll fetch a towel," Lata said as Rianna stepped inside.

"Mum, my hair is not wet. I was in the car. Look, I am dry."

Ignoring her daughter, Lata ushered her into the living room, and then fetched the towel from the upstairs airing cupboard. She ordered Rianna to sit on the floor and dropped the towel onto her head. Lata gave her daughter's hair a good rub. Rianna had to admit, it did feel good.

"Your hair is so dry, dikra," Lata stated when she was finished.

"I told you it wasn't wet."

"When was the last time you put oil in your hair?" Lata tutted then bustled away.

"Now what are you doing?"

In the next few seconds, Lata was back again with a bottle of Indian hair oil. She dolloped a good size into her daughter's hair and began to massage it in.

Rianna relaxed against her mother's knees and closed her eyes. *Okay, this is good.* She let her mother spoil her. Rianna melted into a happy state, the outside forgotten and the warmth of the fireplace consuming her. They had central heating, but her mother had always wanted a feature fireplace. There was no chimney of course; it was all electric nowadays.

"Where is Papa?" she asked.

"He will be home soon. He went to buy a Christmas tree. Really, I don't know what is taking him so long. What shop is open at this hour?"

"Mum, it is only half six and as Christmas is practically on our doorstep, many shops are open until eight. If you stopped watching your Indian shows now and then and stepped out into the real world, you would know what is what. I don't know how you can watch that kind of rubbish, anyway. The same plot goes on for weeks on end. Ouch!"

Lata had slapped Rianna across the head.

"I love my Indian shows, so don't say a bad word against them. It is better than most English shows! Now, go and get changed. Leave the oil in your hair for the whole night. You will have better hair again soon. I am going inside to make the dinner. God knows when your papa will come home, but he will be the first one to bellow for food."

Just as Lata went into the kitchen, the doorbell rang. It was Rajni with a very tall, large, and very real Christmas tree.

"Here, Papa, let me help." Rianna helped her father bring it inside. "Did you forget your keys?"

"It's in my pocket, but my hands were full with the tree. Besides, I knew you all would be home so why bother to use my keys?"

He had a fair point.

"Do you know we didn't really think you would buy a real one," Rianna said.

"By *we*, I assume you mean you and Jia? I am sure the *whole* family will appreciate it, *beta*," said Rajni, smiling. Jia was her seven-year-old sister.

"Are you referring to mum?" she asked.

"Who else?"

They put the tree in front of the double bay window.

Lata came out from the kitchen. "It is a bit big; it will block any light from outside."

"It is dark now, Lata. When the lights and decorations are on, it will look so beautiful," her husband replied drily.

"But tomorrow it will be daytime and the light will be blocked out," Lata argued back.

"Ha!" Rajni waved her protests away.

"No one ever listens to me in this house," Lata grumbled as she went back to the kitchen. Rianna and Rajni laughed silently behind her back. Then there was an excited scream, making them jump.

"A real tree! I can't believe it!" Rianna caught Jia as she came running towards them. "When can we decorate it? Can we do it now? Please?"

"Mum, how long before we eat?" Rianna shouted.

"In an hour," Lata called back.

"Then we can do it now. Let me get changed and then I will get the new decorations out. What do you say?"

"Yes!" squealed Jia.

The family sat together on the sofa staring at the tree. Rianna kept the design the same as the one in her shop, but instead of an angel at the top of the tree, there was the Hindu symbol OM.

"Mummy, it is a Christmas tree, not a Diwali tree," Jia said indignantly.

"We don't put trees up at Diwali," Lata responded.

"But it is a Christmas tree!"

"Why can't a Hindu symbol be part of a Christmas tree, huh? I didn't know there was a rule. I think it looks good and our gods will like it too," smiled Lata.

Jia nodded her head in mock sadness. Rianna caught her eye. Yes, their mother was too much.

"Jia, let it go," Rianna said. "Mum will always win!"

"Okay, let's put the lights on in the room now. I want to watch some TV," said Rajni. He took out a small bag of tobacco from his trouser pocket, took some in his hand and dropped it into his mouth

"Papa!" Rianna reprimanded her father. "People get mouth cancer with that, you know." Rianna always felt compelled to scold her father every time he took out his tobacco, it was a routine now more than anything else.

"Don't you start like your mother. It is good for my particular health. I can't live without it and I only eat a little."

Rianna rolled her eyes.

The TV was on, all eyes turned to the screen. Lata switched to the Bollywood channel, where a new movie was showing. Rianna lost interest and turned to the screen on her phone instead. She saw a WhatsApp message from her friend, Aadi.

Aadi was her best friend from their university days. They studied for a BA in Creative Writing and History together. Her mother didn't approve.

"What kind of job will you get studying that? Will I be the only mother whose children will have mediocre jobs?"

"You know how passionate I am about a career in publishing. And some day, I am going to write a book."

Her mother didn't take to that either.

Everyone thought she and Aadi were in a relationship. Her parents thought so, too, but they didn't mind, they said. It's like that now; arranged marriages are a thing of the past. Except, in Rianna's mind, their relationship was nothing like that. They were simply friends. She read the message. He wanted to go to London with her that weekend. He needed a break from work.

"I'll ask my parents," she texted back.

"You know they will say yes. They like me."

"I'll call you tomorrow, okay? It's only Monday!"

"Is it?" Rianna could hear laughter from his next message.

"Can it be Friday already?"

"Nope." Rianna laughed. She didn't realise it was out loud.

"Sorry," she mumbled, embarrassed when she felt the heat of her mother's gaze on her.

"Can you take your phone upstairs? This film is getting interesting," Lata said, her eyes back on the TV.

Rianna noticed her father had dozed off and her sister had escaped, to her bedroom she suspected, to play on her tablet.

"I'll leave you alone," she whispered. She kissed her mother on the cheek and went upstairs.

Chapter Two

"How are you doing, *beta*? Is it really cold there?" Rianna's aunt, her mother's elder sister, shouted at the phone screen. She was calling from India at ten in the morning, UK time.

"*Maasi*, you don't have to shout. I can hear and see you perfectly well," Rianna said. Jia sniggered next to her.

"Yes, yes, so?"

"So what?" Rianna asked.

"Is it really cold there?"

"It has been snowing on and off for a few days. Quite unusual for December as, for quite a few years, we haven't seen a speck. Why are you asking, *maasi*? Are you planning to come for Christmas?"

Rianna had her fingers crossed. She hoped not. Her *maasi* was very unpredictable and would come to England in a snap.

"No, no. I have to speak to your mother. Where is she? Give her the phone," her *maasi* demanded.

"If she says she wants to come for Christmas, tell her she can't," Rianna whispered to her mum before she passed the phone to her. She had been looking forward to a quiet family Christmas for so long that the thought of her *maasi* turning up filled her with self-pity.

"Lata, are you there?"

"Yes, Rama. I am here. How are you?" Lata sat down on the sofa, Rianna and Jia on each side of her.

"Listen Lata, Damini is getting married. We have found a boy for her."

"Congratulations, that is great news. When is the wedding?"

"It is on Christmas Day. Sorry I can't invite you; it is quite late in the day. Don't mind *na,* it was the decision of her in-laws. They want a quick wedding."

Rianna looked towards the ceiling and thanked God. She didn't quite like her *maasi*—she was an interfering gossip. Her mother had five sisters and two brothers, but this sister was the one Rianna couldn't tolerate, not even a little bit.

"When was the wedding decided, Rama? Have you even had the engagement?" Lata asked. "This is just too quick. You need time to plan a wedding, get the wedding clothes and jewellery, not to mention the catering and decorations…"

"I see you are upset," said Rama. "But it happened so fast. You know Damini is 39 and no one has accepted her for marriage for years. The boy is 42, a bit on the plump side but he is nice. I know he will look after her. He is also a widow, but he has no children. Lata, this was decided last week. Damini found him on Shaadi.com and he came to see us with his mother. I can't be happier, and Damini is happy too."

"Well, I suppose it is good news. God has answered her prayers at last. I just wish I could come and help with the wedding, but we have the shop and we can't close early."

"I didn't expect you to come, don't worry. I wanted to share the news, that's all."

"Give Damini my blessings," said Lata.

"I will. I will get her to give you a video call when she comes back from work."

"Okay."

Lata sat quietly with the phone still in her hand.

"Are you okay, Mum?" asked Rianna. "You seem sad."

"I'm just thinking about Damini. I am happy for her. Finally, she is getting married." Lata looked at Rianna. "What is happening with you and Aadi? Is he going to marry you?"

"Mum! We are just friends, and I don't want to get married, not for a while yet. Don't look at me like that."

It was the look of disappointment—again.

"Uh oh, looks like one of those talks again," Jia said and ran off.

"Ma, do we have to do this again?"

"Do what?"

"Why do you have to bring my marriage up all the time?"

"We don't have to talk about it if you don't want to. You are only twenty-eight, you can make up your own mind. It has nothing to do with me. By now you should be married and have given me grandchildren. But no, nothing to do with me. I'm only your mother. What right do I have to say anything?"

"Ma, you don't need grandchildren. You have Jia, and she is enough."

Lata sniffed. "You know she was not planned, it just happened. Your Papa…"

"Aaagh! I don't want to hear that! Great, now I have a vision of you and Papa… I am going to be sick!"

"Sit down and stop being childish." Lata pulled Rianna down, back to the sofa. "I was going to say your Papa would want to see you married too. That's all."

"One day, I will get married. Just not yet. Look, it's 11 now. I'm meeting Aadi."

"When will you be back?"

"I won't be more than a few hours. We are just catching up—as friends!"

Aadi and Rianna decided to not go down to London that weekend. The weather was still horrendous with blizzards and travelling was not recommended. They decided to meet at a local pub on London Road instead.

The atmosphere was warm and cosy with the full Christmas tree in the corner, complete with the traditional red and green baubles and the silver and gold tinsel. Twinkling fairy lights reflected in clinking glasses of Coke, wine, and pints of beer. Plates of fish & chips, sausages and mash, and lasagne made the rounds to the tables.

"Ah, finally, here is ours," said Aadi, rubbing his hands in delight as a waitress came with their order. Aadi immediately shovelled his food into his mouth as the waitress left.

"Nice," Rianna said.

"What? I am hungry." Typical Aadi.

Rianna chuckled, then cut her fish daintily and popped a piece into her mouth.

"So, this Christmas," he said.

"What about it?"

"I hear you are going to some cottage in the Lake District this year?"

"Who told you that? Oh, Clara. When did you see her?"

"I saw her at Nandos at Freeman's Common. She was waiting to be seated. We got talking and she mentioned it."

"That girl can never keep her mouth shut. I wonder who else she told."

"Does it matter?" Aadi gulped down more beer and Rianna took a sip of her Coke Zero. She didn't feel like having alcohol, even though Aadi had protested.

"I would like to know that what I say to her stays with her. I don't want everyone knowing my business, Aadi."

"Don't be too hard on her, it's just the way she is."

"Oh, Aadi, I think you like her!" Rianna grinned.

"She is not my type. I like… you." Aadi stopped eating and looked at her, really looked at her.

"Oh…" Rianna's mouth opened to reply, but she didn't know what to say. Aadi's words had shocked her to the core. "I… I don't know how to react to that…" She took a deep breath. "Look, you are nice and you are my best friend. I don't want to hurt your feelings…"

"Rianna, hear me out, please. You can make your mind up after that. The thing is, I have liked you since

I met you, but I didn't have the courage to ask you out. But now I have changed, and I believe I have to say something before your mum gets you married." He looked embarrassed, his cheeks flushing just slightly. It was almost cute, but Rianna couldn't think like that. It was Aadi, for goodness sake! She took a long pause before she replied.

"First of all, I am not getting married to anyone for some time. Did you by chance speak to my mother this morning?"

"No."

"Strange, she was talking about that." Rianna shook her head to clear it. "Where was I? Oh yeah, this is getting weird and a bit awkward, too. I... I have to go."

"Will you think about it at least?" Aadi took both her hands in his.

Rianna felt something move in her stomach. It felt like butterflies, which was strange for her. She had never felt anything like this. It made her feel even more confused than she had only seconds before.

"Hello, Earth to Rianna!" Aadi waved a hand in front of her face.

Coming back to the present, and startled, she looked at Aadi and saw him differently. Did she like him too? *Right, enough of this, Rianna. Go home and think. You are not yourself right now.*

"Did you say something, Aadi?" *God, I am confused!*

"I know this is a big shock and you didn't see me coming, but if you can think about it and let me know? Please? I really do like you and believe me when I say this, it has taken me nearly six years to pluck up the courage to tell you how I feel about you."

"Aadi, you are whining."

"Am I? Sorry, I didn't mean to."

"I'll think about... us, okay? If I say I will go out with you, it doesn't mean I am ready to marry. Deal? And before we shake on this, you have to give me until New Year to decide. And you can't tell anyone, especially not my mum!"

Aadi stuck his hand out with a stupid grin on his face. "I promise not to tell anyone. I know you will say yes."

Rianna couldn't help but smile back. She shook his hand to close the deal. This was a territory she wasn't familiar with, but it was on her terms so she didn't mind. Taking a deep breath, she stood up.

"Let's get some air, I know I need it." She flinched as she felt Aadi's hand brushing against hers. "No... don't, Aadi. We are still just friends."

Aadi pushed his hands into his pockets like a sulky teenager. Rianna smiled and put her arm through his. They walked to the car park in silence. The freezing chill was the last thing on Rianna's mind; thoughts of Aadi's declaration of his like for her left her feeling out of sorts, and very confused.

"I'll call you, okay?" she said when they reached their cars, which were parked next to each other.

Aadi stepped forward to kiss her.

"I don't think so," said Rianna, holding a finger up to his face in warning.

"Oh. Okay then."

Rianna and Aadi got into their respective cars and drove away, Rianna feeling a little sad for him. Was it pity?

The fifteenth one, Rianna counted. Aadi had texted her fifteen times. She groaned. Why couldn't he just wait? It can't be that difficult, can it? She text him back.

"Enough, I asked you to wait. Look, I am going to Windermere for Christmas, as you already know. Let me clear my mind and I will talk to you later. Okay? Please just understand."

Three little dots appeared on the screen. He was typing. A moment later, his message popped up.

"You won't take my calls, so I had to text, sorry. I'll leave you alone now. And I hope you will say yes when the time is right for you. Xx."

Two kisses. Huh.

Jia ran into her room and jumped on her bed. "I thought you would be asleep. It's 8.30am and a Saturday." That was Jia, always stating facts. "Who were you texting?"

Rianna put her phone face down on the bedside cabinet.

"Come on then," she said, and Jia gladly crawled in beside her in her double bed. She felt a cool blast of air when the blanket was lifted. Rianna let Jia snuggle up to her. She usually did this when she was curious, was cold, or just wanted a snuggle. Rianna guessed today's reason was curiosity.

"So why are you awake so early on a Saturday? You are normally asleep until 10," Rianna commented.

Ji smiled, her dimpled showing. She looked so cute. "I am so excited because we are going on a Christmas holiday to the lake. Uncle's house is so big. He said he has a heated indoor pool, and a PlayStation, and lots of room everywhere! I am going to ask Papa if I can take my dolls and my make up kit. We will have so much fun!"

Jia was the only girl Rianna knew who loved to play games on the PlayStation, *The Sims*, *Minecraft*, and *Sonic Mania* being her favourites.

"Why do you like playing on the PlayStation? Isn't it a boy's thing?" asked Rianna.

"No, it's for boys *and* girls. Rianna *ben*, what did you do when you were my age?"

"I played outside a lot, things like hopscotch, with ropes, and I had my dolls and my colouring set. I used to read a lot too. Mum complained I couldn't get away from my books, I always had my nose in one!" Rianna's eyes shone as she thought of her childhood. She wished she were Jia's age again, with no complications of men. "And maybe we can take some new Christmas books to the house, what do you say?"

It was so easy to keep her sister entertained for hours. Like her, Jia loved books, too, and she even had her own little library at home.

For the next hour, Rianna read her favourite book, *Matilda*, to Jia. They lost track of time and didn't look up until their mother came in with a basket of ironed clothes.

"Good morning, Mum," Rianna said as she put the book down, ignoring Jia's protest to keep reading. She got up to hug her mother. "I'll put them away."

"Oh, what's all this for?" Lata asked. She wasn't used to hugs from Rianna so this was rare.

"Nothing, I just felt like it." Rianna shrugged.

"It's nice. I like it." Her eyes fell on Jia who was still in the bed, reading *Matilda* alone. "Jia, put that book down and go and brush your teeth, and then have your breakfast. You have your dance class at 11am, remember?"

"I forgot about that. Jia, why didn't you tell me?" Rianna asked.

Jia looked up at both Lata and Rianna. "I don't want to learn dance anymore; I just want to read."

"But you love dancing," said Lata.

"I only go because you make me."

Lata and Rianna looked at one another. Both shared the same expression of surprise.

Rianna sat next Jia on the bed, "Why don't you go today? When you come home, we can talk about it."

"Okay," Jia sighed, and she went to brush her teeth.

"She is such a good dancer. I didn't know she wanted to stop," Lata said.

"You know kids, Mum. They change their minds so many times. I bet she will say she wants to carry on with the classes when she comes back."

"Hmm. So, what are your plans today? Aren't you opening the shop?"

"I open at 11 today… and it's nearly 10! I better get a move on!"

Lata shook her head and carried on with the morning housework.

"I've already made tea for you," she said.

"Thanks Mum!"

Rianna went about her morning schedule—even though it was late—Aadi and the problem forgotten completely.

Chapter Three

Rianna opened the shutters and unlocked the door to the shop. Today, she was hosting a book signing for a brilliant children's book writer, Tania Twiddlesticks. She had met her on several occasions; she was a bit eccentric, but her books sold. Her titles included *The Witch and the Bag*, *Mr. and Mrs. Toad's Wedding*, and Rianna's all-time favourite, *The Witch's Flying Car and her Adventures*. Her new title was *The Witch and Mrs. Toad's Christmas Party*.

"How did you get her to come to your shop if she is so famous? Wouldn't she go to the bigger bookshops?" her dad asked her when they were in the garden one beautiful summer's day. He was gardening and she was drawing flowers in her sketchbook.

"I got lucky. Tania is booked months in advance. But one day she came across my small shop, and she fell in love with it. She said and I quote, 'It is so idyllic and personal. And cosy! I've been looking for a place like this in the middle of nowhere—'"

"In the middle of nowhere!" Rajni interrupted. "We live in Leicester, not in the middle of bloody nowhere!"

"Anyway, as I was saying," Rianna said, choosing to ignore her dad's language, "she said there was a certain charm about my shop she hadn't felt anywhere before. She said her new book was coming out in December and asked if I wouldn't mind hosting a book signing. I was ecstatic and so of course I said yes."

Tania Twiddlesticks got her publicist to arrange the afternoon and even offered to pay for the food and drinks. She had a poster designed and the flyers done just for this event.

Rianna sighed happily. She checked her watch, it was coming to 11.30 now, where was Clara? There was lots to do before the families came at 4.30. Super excited, she began without her friend. A few baubles had fallen off the tree so she picked them up and put them back on. She saw her reflection in the silver one she was still holding and sagged at the sight of herself.

She looked run-down, her skin had the pallidness that winter always brought, and she had dark circles under her eyes. To make matters worse, her hair had grown out to below her shoulders and her layers had gone. *I must make an appointment with the hairdressers.* She hung the bauble back on the tree, not looking at herself again. *Might even get my nails done. Why not? It is Christmas.* The thought made her feel better.

The shop needed a bit of dusting and the area where the talk was going to be would need to be cleared. Then, there was food and drink to organise. She had bought the cakes and biscuits in advance and stored them away. For the children, as it was coming to Christmas, she had made up little presents of a book and a cuddly toy. There was going to be so much excitement, she couldn't wait. She even had her dad dropping Jia before he went to the tool shop. Mum was busy, something about Mrs. Jain coming to see her that afternoon; she had some problems apparently. *When doesn't she have problems?*

The bell clanged and Clara came in. She wore a bright red coat and looked chic with her red bobble hat, her black gloves, and her long boots.

"Good morning," she sang. "Isn't it a lovely day, even if it is freezing out there like a massive, overworked freezer."

"Or like the Antarctic," said Rianna.

"Yes! Like at the Antarctic!"

Rianna laughed silently. "So, how was your weekend?"

"My brother announced he is going travelling after Christmas. He decided to take a gap year from uni. Mum was dead upset, you know. She said kids get kidnapped, killed, and/or get arrested abroad. Do you know, that is why Mum never goes abroad on holiday? The other reason is because we can't simply afford it, of course."

"I don't see why not, doesn't she work?"

"She works at Tesco, gets a fair wage I suppose. But since my brother and I moved out, she stops getting rent from us. My dad doesn't help now that he is with his floosy girlfriend, who is super rich. They live in a mansion in the countryside. I visited them one weekend, the house has a massive pool, a jacuzzi and even a games room. So lucky."

"My uncle has a pool too at the house in Windermere. I can't wait to relax when we go there for Christmas. The family go away on trips quite regularly and he lets the house out."

"Ooo, is it a holiday home then? Sounds amazing."

"Not quite, they live there but he hates to leave his properties empty and rents them out when they are all away. He does this on recommendation only, though. For example, if I gave him your name, he would be happy to give you the keys. He has rules though, like no smoking, parties are limited to ten people, and the house must be kept clean and tidy when you leave. He takes a deposit too."

"That seems fair. Can you ask when the next time he will let it out will be? It would be a great break for me and Michael. God do we need it, as long as it's not too expensive."

"Sure, now come on. We'd better get the shop prepared for the event. We've wasted enough time already."

The event went ahead smoothly. Rianna couldn't be more delighted. Twenty families were booked on the talk, the children squealed and laughed throughout the reading, and they became even more excited when the presents and food came out. Clara arranged some colouring stations and a play table for the children, while Rianna liaised with the adults.

"What a good idea," said one lady. "We can eat in peace for a while."

Tania was dressed as the witch from her book. She had a soft cuddly toy toad stitched onto her black robe on the shoulder. Her stockings had red and gold stripes. She was a sight to see, and the children loved it all.

"Thank you for this opportunity," Rianna said as Tania got up to leave.

"Oh, it wasn't me who made this afternoon a success, it was your lovely, charming self. You and your assistant have worked so hard.

I love the decorations, the Christmas tree, and the food, too. You have gone to town with this one. I've already told my friends and my editor about this spectacular place. You'll be getting more business soon, and so many Christmas invites, too." Tania winked.

Tania left soon after, for she had another engagement. Rianna, however, felt she had made a new friend for life.

"What a turnout!" Clara gushed. "And *she* talked to me and signed my book!"

"That was the plan, Clara," Rianna said dryly. "It's been a long day. Come on, let's clear up and go home. Can't believe it is seven already."

Rianna usually closed at six for the customers. She worked on her accounts the same day before going home, but she was too tired. The event had taken a lot out of her. Poor Jia fell asleep in the backseat of the car as they drove back.

"Don't worry about dropping me off today," Clara said. "Michael is picking me up; we are going to that Turkish restaurant that just opened. I am going to mention the Windermere getaway."

"Great! Have a nice evening," said Rianna.

Rianna carried Jia to the door when they reached home.

"Take her straight upstairs to her bedroom," Rajni said. "Looks like you both had a good time."

"We did, she loved it!" Rianna said in a low tone so as not to wake her sister up.

When she came back downstairs, she sat beside her father.

"Where is Mum?" she asked.

"She is upstairs, something about sarees and organising," Rajni replied. "The dinner is ready, it's only you and me eating. Lata ate already; today she is fasting. And then you can tell me everything about your event and don't leave anything out. Did you get a lot of pictures?"

"Yes Papa, I have posted them on my social media already. Didn't you see it?"

Rajni and Rianna warmed the chapatis, the potato curry, the daal and rice, and sat down to eat in front of the TV. Rianna loved talking to her dad. He was always interested in her bookshop and in her life. He didn't badger her about marriage or ask if she had a boyfriend. He let her be.

For the rest of the evening, Rianna spent time cuddled up to her dad on the sofa watching a comedy on Netflix. Her mum was still upstairs organising her saris.

"Hurry Rianna, is the table set out?" Lata shouted from the kitchen.

"Why are you so tense, Mum? They said they will be here at six, and it's only five. And you know how they are, always much later than they say."

Rajni chuckled from behind his paper. "Your mother will never learn."

Meenakshi, Lata's younger sister, was coming to dinner with her husband and their grown-up children, Jay and Anaya. They were twins. Rianna liked them and they had become close in recent years, since they left their teens. Her aunt lived in Muswell Hill, in London, and they had two Labradors. Rianna and Jia wanted a dog of their own but never got one.

"Absolutely not, never in this house!" Lata had said in a loud voice when Jia asked for one Sunday, when everyone was having a traditional English fry-up. "I have enough people to look after in this house, I will not add more living things to my family."

"I can't believe you said that. We are your family!" exclaimed Rianna.

"You know what I mean. You'll get bored of George, and then your Papa or I will have to walk him."

"So, we are getting a dog named George?" asked Jia, excited.

"Hmm. No."

"That means yes," Jia whispered to Rianna. They high fived behind their mother's back.

"I heard that!"

The sisters giggled.

The doorbell rang and Rajni opened the door to Meenakshi and her family.

"Come in, come in. Lata has been waiting on tenterhooks," he said as they all trooped inside. After taking their shoes and coats off and putting them in the appropriate places, they filed into the living room with boxes of Christmas presents.

"Meenakshi, late as usual," Lata tutted as she hugged her sister.

"Sorry," Meenakshi said. "It is the kids and Peter. They made me late. Where is the Christmas tree?"

Rianna's *maasi* married a white man. Her grandmother didn't approve but her grandfather accepted him. It was the seventies, a time when interracial marriages were frowned upon. And they still are.

However, her *maasi* didn't care and married Peter anyway. Rianna liked him.

"Don't listen to a word she says, Lata. You know why we are late," Peter laughed. He took the presents and put them under the tree.

Lata smiled knowingly. Meenakshi wouldn't leave the house unless it was spotless and she was dressed to perfection.

"It was the traffic." Meenakshi smiled back. Her cheeks turned red; she knew she had been caught out.

"Anyway, it doesn't matter," Lata said quickly. "Rianna, let's get the food warmed and then we can eat. Children, look at you, so tall and grown up!"

Rianna hugged her cousins.

"It's good to see you after so long. You don't even text anymore. You do know WhatsApp is free, right?" Rianna said as he followed her into the kitchen.

"Sorry," said Jay. "Life got busy, I guess."

"Jay! Come and talk to your uncle, he has a proposition for you," Peter called out from the living room.

"Actually, he is having problems at work," his sister, Anaya, said conspiratorially, once he had left the room.

"Oh?"

"It's about his boss and she is a lady. Long story. We are here for a few days. I'll fill you in later when we are alone," said Anaya.

Everyone sat down to eat. Jia sat next to Anaya and chatted all the way. Jay and Rianna sat next to each other. She could feel he was troubled so she didn't ask probing questions.

"Ah Rianna," said Meenakshi. "How is business? Your mother tells me you have an admirer."

"Mum!" It was Rianna's turn to blush but not of embarrassment. "I told you, Aadi is just a friend!"

"Okay, okay, let's talk about something else," Rajni said nervously.

There was a tense moment, and then Peter laughed. Everyone looked at him like he was mad.

"I just remembered, I think we left the house lights on, love!"

Chapter Four

Meenakshi got off the phone to her neighbours and sat back down at the table again.

"It's okay now," she said. "Joginder said he will turn off the lights. Thank God we gave him our key."

"But how do you know he won't steal anything from our house?" Jay pointed out.

"*Chup*! He is always suspicious. Joginder is a good man."

"Mum, I think he is a bit too friendly; don't you think? Should dad be worried?" Anaya laughed.

"I have the most rude and ungrateful children in the world!"

Rianna caught everyone trying hard not to laugh. Her *maasi* was melodramatic, as usual.

"No one loves me," Meenakshi sniffed.

"Come on, Mum. We are just having a laugh," Jay said. "If Joginder did have a crush on you, Dad can handle him. Can't you Dad?"

"Sure, I can. I wouldn't let anyone take my darling wife," Peter said. He put his arm around Meenakshi and pulled her into him.

"Why can't you be romantic like that?" Lata asked her husband.

"I bought you a real Christmas tree, didn't I?" Rajni said.

"That was for the girls, not for me. When was the last time you were romantic, huh?"

This, Rianna wanted to hear. She could see her father thinking very hard.

"Well?" Lata prompted.

"I'm still thinking, dear," said Rajni. "…Oh, I know, it was on our wedding anniversary. I took you to a romantic holiday to Paris."

"Rianna practically threw us out of the house. She paid for the holiday as a present and she insisted we go. It was hardly his idea," Lata told everyone.

"And you two were so stubborn, wanting to take me and Jia with you. Remember Mum, when you said, 'What will I do with your father, all alone in a strange city where they eat odd food?'" said Rianna.

"But you came back, refreshed and happier. Papa, you and Mum should go on more trips together."

"That we should, I agree wholeheartedly." Rajni took a sip of his wine.

Rianna was thankful the conversation had diverted from her and Aadi. It was something she didn't want to even think about. Anaya smiled at her and she smiled back, lifting her spirits. She was sure she would ask questions when they were alone tomorrow. She stifled a yawn.

Lata and Meenakshi began to talk about their family in India, and Rajni and Peter talked about cricket and other sports. Soon, with dinner finished, the girls helped with the cleaning and tidying up. Jiya roped Jay into playing on her PlayStation with her, which he seemed to

be enjoying whilst the men took their conversation to the living room.

Rianna stared at the living room ceiling, unable to sleep. On one side of her was Jia and on the other side was Anaya. Jay slept in Jia's bed, and Meenakshi and Peter slept in Rianna's double bed.

Jia was curled up to Rianna, muffled up in her Disney printed sleeping bag, which she insisted on sleeping in. "Just like as if we are camping," she'd said.

"Rianna?" Anaya whispered, breaking into her thoughts.

"Was I thinking too loud? Did I wake you?" Rianna said.

"No, I was awake already, it's just that I'm not used to sleeping in a living room on a hard mattress."

"What makes you think I like it? I miss my bed."

"I have a boyfriend," Anaya blurted out. "I wanted to tell you before but didn't get a chance."

"So, that's what this is about. Go on, tell me."

"He is not Indian."

"There's nothing wrong in that, is it? You are half-English, remember. But if it bothers you then you shouldn't be with him."

"It's not that. I like the fact but what gets to me is that he is a mummy's boy. And his mum doesn't like me. And he is American too."

"American, wow. What is he doing here then?"

"He is here on a work visa; he's the manager of a London hotel. One of the best chains actually."

"So, you are worried that he is a mummy's boy. I presume his mum is here in the UK?"

"His mum is not here but one day we did a video call. I just have a feeling she doesn't like me. Like you know when you get goosebumps when something evil is near you? Like that."

Rianna didn't know she even had a boyfriend. "When did you meet him exactly? How long have you been going out with him?"

"A week."

"What!" Rianna shouted. Jia stirred. "Oops."

When Jia was back in the land of nod, Rianna got up and motioned Anaya to follow her into the kitchen. The counter tops were immaculate, and everything was in its place. Lata hated things put where they weren't supposed to be put.

"Do you want some hot chocolate or tea? I know I need something," Rianna said. Anaya nodded and Rianna set about making some spiced chai for both of them and put some snacks on the table.

"Anaya, you have been seeing a man for one week only and you are unhappy… are you pregnant?"

"No, of course not. I mean, we have had sex and everything, but that's all. We have been safe. The thing is, I want to go to the US with him on a small holiday. He asked me to go with him."

"It sounds fishy to me, if you want my opinion." Rianna poured the hot piping chai into two large mugs, then handed one to Anaya. She blew on hers and took a sip. It was good, it calmed her. "Right Anaya, listen. You haven't known this man long enough to go on a holiday abroad, or even anywhere for a start. He could have a family back there, and perhaps he just wants to—and this is the worst-case scenario—kidnap you, lock you up in a hut in the middle of nowhere, and do wicked things!"

"Are you making fun of me?"

Rianna was laughing, but she composed herself. "Look, you and this man only met a week ago. It is pretty premature for him to ask you to go on a holiday, don't you think? Just be careful, that's all I'm saying."

"I suppose you're right."

"Have you told anyone else about this? Have you told Jay?"

"He is too immersed in his own life to be concerned about my life. Remember, I told you about his boss and girlfriend?"

"You did. What's the story there?"

"Jay is infatuated with this woman; I think she takes advantage of him."

The girls talked all night, only going to sleep at five in the morning, leaving their mugs in the sink.

"Wake up, wake up!" Jia shouted.

"What time is it?" Rianna groaned. Anaya pulled the duvet over her head. "Will you stop shouting and pull the curtains closed."

"But mummy is making hot *parothas* and she told me to wake you up so you could help her in the kitchen."

"Why is Jia shouting?" Anaya sat up, her hair tousled and all over the place.

Rianna yawned. "What time is it?"

"Mummy, what time is it?" Jia shouted

"Nine-thirty!"

Rianna and Anaya got up and went upstairs to shower and brush their teeth, feeling the pain of their all-nighter.

"Good morning," Rajni greeted them cheerily as he met them at the top of the staircase.

It would be a good morning to you, since you slept in your own bed! Rianna smiled weakly at her father. *But it's my own fault, too. No one told me to stay up talking all night.*

"Morning, Papa."

"Good morning, Uncle," said Anaya.

"Didn't you sleep well last night? It's those mattresses isn't it? We must replace them," he said. He sniffed, then rolled his eyes in delight. "Is your mother making *parothas*?"

"I think so," yawned Rianna.

"She's a gem! I love a hot breakfast; your auntie makes them all the time, Anaya."

Rianna and Anaya joined the rest of the family at the breakfast table.

"Papa, I'm going into the shop today," she said as she helped herself to the food and chai.

"It's Sunday, *dikra*. You knew your *maasi* was coming today. Can't Clara look after it for you?" asked Lata.

"It's the busiest season, Mum. You know that. I don't have a choice really. Clara is already there." Rianna turned to Anaya. "We open at 11 officially— you know, Sunday trading." She checked her watch; it was creeping up to 10am. "I'd better get a move on!"

"But *beta*, your breakfast?" Meenakshi said. "You can't go on an empty stomach!"

"I'll eat when I come back after work. Actually, Anaya, Jay, do you want to come a bit later on? Papa can drop you off," said Rianna.

"What will I do at a bookshop? I don't read," Jay scoffed.

"I'll come," said Anaya. "I love bookshops! You are so lucky to own one."

Rianna beamed. The bookshop was her lifeline, and she didn't know what she'd do without it.

"Do you know what we need in here?" Rianna said as she unboxed some more Christmas decorations.

"What?" Clara and Anaya said together.

"Christmas music, that's what. Without seasonal music, the bookshop feels empty. Luckily for us, I have a CD player somewhere in the back and a Christmas CD from last year."

"But it's not even the middle of December. Isn't it a little bit too early?" Clara put in her two pence worth of negativity.

"I sometimes wonder about you, you know. How can you not get into the Christmas spirit? This is one of the best times of the year. The music, the tinsel, the candles, the tree, the presents, I could go on. I just feel all fuzzy and warm when I think about it."

"She is definitely on drugs," Clara said to Anaya, who giggled.

"And you're always miserable," snapped Rianna as she stormed into the back room.

Rianna loved Clara, she really did, but sometimes her negativity really annoyed her. She knew Clara had problems at home, but need she bring them back here? *Am I being too harsh and inconsiderate? I should be more sympathetic. It is supposed to be the season of giving and loving, after all.* Rianna sighed as she opened the cupboard.

She came back with the CD player and plugged it into the socket, then popped the CD in and pressed play. The shop was engulfed in Mariah Carey's *All I want for Christmas*. Rianna took Clara to one side.

"Sorry for being Miss Nasty, Clara. I didn't mean it. Look, is everything fine at home?"

"Yeah, of course. Why are you being odd and clingy?" Clara gave Rianna a strange look, who in return gave her a tight hug.

"I'm here for you, always."

"Oh, I know you are, silly. Come on, let's put fake snow around the book displays and the window display, and spray some white on the window, too. And do you still have the cute Christmas village? We can make space on the other window and put it there."

"Oh, I knew you didn't hate Christmas!" Rianna laughed.

The village wasn't exactly small. With Anaya's help, they got it down from the shop attic and began to build it. It was so much fun. They placed the clock tower in the middle and the park around it. A beautiful little Christmas tree twinkled with tiny baubles that lit up. Anaya placed figures of the children and adults around the green, and Clara put the houses together on one side of the display. On the other side was a hill, where some figures sleighed down on mats. Last of all, fake snow was added. It was truly mesmerising.

"We have a Christmas village at home too, but it's smaller," Anaya said. "Mum doesn't let me help her put it out. She says it is her project."

"That's nice," said Clara wistfully. "They are so expensive. We can't afford one."

Rianna smiled, knowing instantly what Christmas gift she was going to give to Clara.

"What are you doing this Christmas, Anaya?" Clara asked as they moved away from the display and admired their work.

"My dad's side are coming to join us. There will be about twenty or thirty of us, depending who turns up."

"Blimey!" Clara exclaimed. "Do you have the space?"

"We live in quite a big house," said Anaya. "So, I think we should be okay."

Clara was gobsmacked. "You two live in a different world to me, that's for sure. I live in a flat with my Mum. We can just about manage five people."

"You are welcome to come to ours on Christmas day," Rianna volunteered. She kicked herself. How could she be so stupid! She quickly backtracked. "Not this year though. We are going to the Lake District, remember? I told you. Sorry."

"It doesn't matter. Mum and I will have a great time, just the two of us."

Did Rianna see a shadow of sadness pass through her friend's face?

Chapter Five

Rianna stopped at the florist window, admiring the Christmas flower arrangement. It was so beautiful. The foliage spray, red berries, the ruby mini magnolia picks, and silver glitter against a backdrop of pine and green foliage gave her a seasonal tingle. It was a new shop that opened just last week.

"Good morning." The shop assistant greeted her with a smile.

"Good morning," said Rianna. "I saw your lovely flower arrangement in the window—the Christmas one. I would like to order two, please."

"Aren't they lovely? Jessica—she's my manager—and I made that one up yesterday and you are our first customer to buy one."

"That's great," said Rianna.

The lady wasn't finished talking. "Every Christmas arrangement comes with a complimentary box of chocolates and a Christmas card—it's an ideal Christmas gift. Did you say you wanted two?"

"I did," replied Rianna. "How much are they?"

"One hundred and ten pounds each," the lady said proudly.

Rianna nearly dropped her coffee. "How much?"

"It is a reasonable price, right? And as I said, it will be a perfect gift. Who doesn't like flowers, chocolates, and cards? So, do you want to put in an order?"

Not for that price, Rianna thought. She wasn't being Scrooge but she couldn't justify spending that much on flowers, even if it was Christmas.

"I'll think about it," she said quickly.

"Oh, are you sure?"

"Well, no, I think I will look around. Thanks anyway," said Rianna.

The lady looked alarmed. "Wait, let me see what I can do for you. Don't go away, I'll be back soon." Five minutes later, she was back. "Jessica said we can do you a very special price as you are buying two. The chocolates and the cards are still complementary."

"Okay, what is the new price?"

"We can do it for £100 each."

"I can get one for a reasonable £75," Rianna stated. She was bluffing of course; she didn't know if she really could. But she was curious to see if the sales lady would back down to that price.

"Huh huh, wait a moment." She disappeared but quickly came back again. "Jessica has agreed to do them for £75 each. Shall I make them up for you to collect later?" she said.

"Yes please. Actually, do you deliver?"

"Yes, if the address is in Leicestershire it is £4.95 and if it is outside, it is £9.99. Where do you want them to be delivered?"

"I just want one to be delivered. It is for a good friend of mine."

"A special friend, like a boyfriend?" The lady's face lit up.

"No," laughed Rianna. Aadi came to her mind but she quickly dismissed it. "Actually, she is an author. You may have heard of her, Tania Twiddlesticks, the author of children's books."

"Oh, I love all her books. I read them to my daughter. I can't believe I know someone who knows a famous author personally! How did you become friends?"

"We are colleagues more than friends. She did a talk at my bookshop, which is on the corner of this road."

"I'll come and check it out."

"That would be lovely. I sell refreshments as well as books. And I'll do you a special price when you buy a book, too, since you did me a good deal on the flowers."

The lady laughed. "I'm Clarice."

"Nice to meet you. I am Rianna. Right, I'd better be off." She quickly wrote the address to where she wanted the flower arrangement to be delivered. "Can I ask when it will be delivered?"

Clarice flicked through her A4 calendar. "We have a slot at the weekend. I see she lives in Loughborough, so the charge will be £4.95."

Rianna paid the extra. "What time can I pick up the second arrangement?"

"As you are literally down the road, I can drop it off. That way I can see your shop. Say four o'clock?"

"Perfect. See you then."

It was snowing again, making the dark evening enchanting. The weatherman predicted snow for two weeks and then there would be a lull, but it was looking like this year they would get a real white Christmas. The government was ready for it— miraculously! This year, they had already arranged salt trucks to grit motorways and major haul roads. Tool and DIY shops were selling out of shovels, de-icers, scrapers, and sledges. No one had seen snow like this in Leicester for a good few years. Everyone was excited, especially Jia.

Rianna felt she truly was in Narnia. She watched the silent snow fall, mesmerised by its beauty.

"Hello! Earth to Rianna!" Clara waved a book in front of her. "Is anyone at home?"

Rianna jumped and turned away from the window. "It's so enchanting outside, don't you think?"

"Have you been reading children's fantasy stories again? It's snowing, Rianna. That to me means it's bloody cold and that I should be in my pjs, sitting by the fire, and watching Christmas reruns."

"Or we could go sleighing in Bradgate park? I'll bet a lot of people will be there this year with their sledges. You know what, I think I'll do that. I'll take Jia with me. Why don't you come too? I'll buy you lunch afterwards. It will be so much fun!"

"Why not, hey? I'm up for a bit of fun and I know I am long overdue in that department. As it happens, I have two old sledges in the garage. Mind you, I'll have to dig it up from all the junk we have in there. I'll ask Mum."

"And I have one in my shed. Still new. We bought for Jia last year but sadly we got no snow."

The last customer left and then it was just Rianna and Clara. Clara began to clear the tables of cups and plates whilst Rianna checked the sales of the day on the computer. Takings were good. The Christmas season always brought a boost against the competition of online book retailers. She was blessed. She heard the bell clang, and she looked up from the screen. It was Clarice.

"Hello," Clarice said to Clara. "I have a delivery for Rianna. Is this her shop?"

"It certainly is," said Rianna, getting up from her seat. "Clara, this is Clarice. She works at the florist down the road." Rianna took the flower arrangement from Clarice.

"These flowers aren't for me, they are for you, Clara." She presented the arrangement to her best friend. "Just a thank you and one of many Christmas presents from me. Merry Christmas!"

"Wow. These are beautiful!" Clara read the card and took out the box of Dairy Milk chocolates. "They look so expensive."

"You deserve it, silly. After all the hard work you put into the place and for being such a good friend to me.

"But I can't afford to give you anything so extravagant."

"I'm not expecting anything from you. If you want to give me something, make sure it is small and inexpensive, okay?"

Clara sniffed. She put the flowers down on the counter and hugged Rianna. "No one has ever done something so nice for me."

There was a cough and the girls turned to Clarice, suddenly remembering she was there.

"I better get going back to the shop. Still got lots to do," she said.

"Thanks for delivering these," Rianna said. "Please come again and browse something. I haven't forgotten my promise.

Clarice said goodbye and left.

"Do you know, Rianna, I love you."

"Now, you are going to make me cry. Come here." Rianna and Clara hugged one another.

"Rianna, do you mind if I left the flowers here? Mum will only throw them away or she'll make me do it. She says the smell of flowers give her a headache. I know she isn't allergic."

"How do you know?"

"We got her tested when she complained of severe headaches. As it happened, it wasn't flowers that did it, it was from the prescription painkillers she was taking for her joints. The doctor changed the prescription, but she'll still throw the flowers away, and I can't let that happen to Mrs. Christmas, can I?"

"Mrs. Christmas?" Rianna raised an eyebrow.

"Yes, I just named her. I'll put her in a vase upstairs."

Upstairs was their little staff room where they ate their lunch and relaxed. Rianna had put in a comfy two-seater, a microwave, a kettle, and some dishes and cutlery. Clara went upstairs with the flowers and Rianna went back to the computer.

As Rianna predicted, Bradgate Park was paced with couples, families, and teens. Small children shrieked, laughed, and screamed as they sledged down the snow-covered hills in their wellies, warm coats, hats, gloves, and scarves.

Rianna spotted an elderly couple sledge down and fall sideways as they reached the bottom, their cheeks rosy red from the biting cold but their eyes full of merriment.

"Isn't that lovely?" she said to Clara. "When I get married someday, I would like to have a relationship like they have."

"So, you *do* plan to marry?" asked Clara. "I thought you were against it."

"I am," she protested, but then softer, she added, "but not forever."

"Hello, so this is Rianna, is it?" Clara's mum, Jane, came up behind them. "You could have waited for me, Clara."

Lata and Jia reached them at the same time.

"It is cold," said Lata.

"Well, you insisted on coming," said Rianna. "Don't complain."

"Kids these days, no resect!" Lata tutted.

"I agree with you. Clara doesn't show me an ounce of respect," said Jane.

"I do!" declared Clara.

"Rianna *ben*, can we have a go now? I am tired of waiting." Jia tugged on Rianna's coat sleeve.

Their mother insisted on Jia calling Rianna '*ben*,' meaning sister, as the age gap between them was eighteen years. "It also shows respect," Lata had said.

"Okay, let's go." Rianna took Jia's gloved hand.

"Yes! Come on Clara *ben*!"

"Oh, you called me *ben*. You are so cute, I could gobble you up!" Clara squeezed Jia.

"I am not food, Clara *ben*," Jia said haughtily.

Clara roared with laughter.

"Come on, before the snow begins to melt," Jia said.

Lata and Jane looked up at the sky. "Not likely," they said together, and then looked at each other, laughing.

"Hello, I'm Jane." Jane extended a hand.

"I am Lata."

"It's nice to see them talking, and giving each other company," Rianna said as she, Clara, and Jia climbed up the hill, dragging the sledges behind them.

"Agreed. It would be awkward otherwise." Clara breathed hard. "Gosh, I do need to go to the gym. Why did you make me get like this?"

"That is hardly my fault." Rianna also struggled to breath. "Let's join the gym again after Christmas. I need to get fit too."

The blue sky vanished to be replaced by a totally white one. Flakes flurried from the sky.

"Rianna *ben*, let's go down the hill now!"

"But we are only half-way up," said Rianna.

"It's not a bad idea." Clara stopped climbing. "I don't think I can make it to the top anyway. My back is killing me, and my asthma is playing up."

"You don't have asthma."

"Don't I? I feel like I could be asthmatic."

Rianna saw flattish spot not far up. "Let's sledge down from there then."

As they reached the spot, they each got on their sledges. They sped down the steep hill, swerving other sledgers and avoiding small rocks. Jia was a pro at it, coming to a stop at the bottom at the same time as Rianna, with Clara a few seconds behind.

"I want to go again! But this time, can I sit with you Rianna *ben*?" Jia, excited, jumped up and down.

"Sure but let me catch my breath first. Steering is hard work!"

"That was so much fun!" said Clara.

Lata and Jane came to the girls.

"Ah, there you are. We are cold, let's go home," said Lata. "I can't feel my fingers and toes." She shivered.

"I second that," said Jane, rubbing her arms. "I wouldn't have come if I knew it was going to snow. I'd love a nice cup of tea with a biscuit right now."

Jia looked disappointed. "Please, just one last one?"

"One last one then," smiled Rianna.

The snow was coming down fast now, but she didn't want to disappoint her little sister.

Five minutes later, and the three girls were flying down the hill again but this time, Rianna and Jia shared a sledge. Thank God it was big enough, but Rianna couldn't see a thing as snow grew thick and fierce, coating her glasses in a fine white dust.

"Watch out!" Rianna heard Clara shout but it was too late. Jia screamed and then the sledge toppled over, throwing Rianna and Jia off. Jia rolled down the hill before Rianna could stop her.

Somewhere, she heard another scream.

"Jia! Where are you?" Rianna shouted.

"I've got her!" came Clara's voice from somewhere. "We are near the big tree. Can you see it?"

Rianna saw a tall shadow of a tree amidst the falling snow, and two crouched shadows. She found Jia holding her leg. She was grinning.

"Are you okay?" Rianna asked.

"That was wicked! Look, one of my teeth came out! Ouch!"

"What is it?"

"I think she may have broken her leg," said Clara.

"Oh no, are you okay, Jia? We'll get you to A&E, don't worry. I'm so sorry, I should have been more careful!" Rianna took off her scarf and gently put it around Jia's leg.

"Help me get her on the sledge. I'll pull her to the carpark and take her straight to the hospital. Mum's going to kill me!"

"I can't wait to tell everyone at school about this!" Jia said happily.

"How can your sister be happy? I bet she is an alien. Most kids her age would be crying," said Clara.

Rianna and Clara trudged back to the Lata and Jane, with Jia in tow mode.

Chapter Six

"I really can't believe you," Lata said for the umpteenth time. "Couldn't you be careful? My poor sweet Jia." Lata sniffed.

"I'm sorry! It was an accident," Rianna said. She felt a prickle of guilt across her chest. "But it was snowing hard, and I couldn't see properly."

They were headed home with Jia in a leg cast. She was lucky. She escaped with just a few scratches and a fixable leg, and nothing else, the doctor said. She seemed stern when she spoke. "Playing in the snow or sledging is so dangerous, in my opinion it shouldn't be allowed." She turned to Lata. "Keep her leg elevated and keep the cast dry. If you see any severe swelling, come back to A&E. Check her skin daily and avoid applying lotions or powders."

She gave a gentle smile to Jia. "Your leg will get itchy but don't scratch the inside of the cast with any object. Mum can give you a paracetamol if you are in a lot of pain. You know what, I think you are a superhero, you didn't cry once! It must be one of your special powers."

Jia beamed, and the doctor gave her a lollipop.

"Does this mean I don't have to go to school on Monday?" Jia asked Lata when she was back in her room and in her bed.

"We'll see how you go, but the doctor did give you crutches so I don't see a reason why you can't." Lata soothed her hair.

Rianna took her sister's hand in hers. "I'm sorry, Jia."

"Why? I think we had fun today!"

Rianna laughed. Once Jia was comfortable, Rianna and her mother went downstairs. It was 4pm by then—and dark. Rajni was still at work. Lata bustled to the kitchen and made two mugs of chai.

"Thanks, Mum," said Rianna when her mother came to the living room and placed the mugs on the coffee table.

"Hmm. It was a good thing nothing happened to you, too. I can thank God for that at least."

Rianna had a feeling this incident would be told over and over again to all her extended family, both here in the UK and abroad.

"Well, they didn't have TV back then, what else were my grandparents to do?" Lata said boldly when Rianna asked her about the size of their family one day.

And now she had a new tale to tell.

"You're thinking about me, aren't you? You are worried I will tell the whole family what you did today, am I right?"

"How did you know I was thinking that?" Rianna was gobsmacked.

"I am your mother, don't underestimate what I can and can't do. Now, did you tell your father about Jia's accident, like I told you to?"

"I tried, but he didn't answer. Besides, I didn't want to worry him."

Rajni worked part time at his friend's garage.

"My father taught me everything there was to know about cars, and how to fix them. He even said I was good at it," said had Rajni when he had taken the job. "But I wanted to be an accountant. I liked numbers. At the moment, my friend needs my help so that's all I'm doing, on alternate Saturdays." Rajni liked to explain things to his family.

"Well, what are you waiting for? Ring him again and if he doesn't pick up, text him."

That was exactly what Rianna did. She texted her dad in the end.

Nothing to worry about. Jia has broken her leg. We took her to A&E. She is home now. All good. Rianna.

In the next minute or so, Rajni called.

"What happened?"

"She is okay, Papa." Rianna quickly relayed the day's events. "I was careless."

"I'm coming home now. But are you okay? Were you hurt, too?"

Trust her dad to worry about her as well.

"I'm absolutely fine, Papa."

"Right, I'm coming home."

Rajni made a huge fuss over Jia. He asked her many times if she was okay. He was surprised when he found her happy, playing on her tablet. He sat with her for a long time until she told him to go away; she'd had enough of him and just wanted something to eat.

"Can I have some chocolate?"

Rajni roared with laughter.

"I'm looking for a kitten. A house cat actually."
Rianna and Clara stopped at a second-hand bookshop.
The window display was pretty, with books
surrounded by Christmas decorations and twinkly
lights.

"Why?" Clara asked. "I thought you mum didn't
want pets in her house?"

"Who said it was for us?"

"Isn't it?"

"Just kidding, of course it's for us. Really for Jia.
House cats are good pets, they don't go outside and
come back with stinky dead mice, or a half-eaten
pigeon. My next-door neighbour's cat did that to
them once. I was there at the time; it was disgusting!"

"But your mum still won't like it," Clara
emphasised.

"Then she will have to live with it. Anyway, this is
for Jia."

"You mean you want to stop feeling guilty." Clara raised an eyebrow.

"That, too." Rianna entered the bookshop. It was full of stuffed bookshelves and boxes of old collectibles books, new and used, old leather-bound and cloth-bound volumes, and magazines.

"It's like a treasure trove in here!" Clara began rummaging through a box, exclaiming at every title she came across. "I want them all!"

"Fun fact. Do you know this shop has been here since the early 1900s?" Rianna said. "I know, I'm a nerd. Anyway, coming back to the kitten, I want to get one as soon as possible, but not from a pet shop. Do you know anyone?"

"I'll ask a friend. She usually knows. You could search on Gumtree for cat breeders?"

"I'll check on there, but if you could ask your friend as well...."

"Yep, no probs. Oh look, I found a very rare copy of *Little Women*."

"How do you know it's rare?" Rianna came round to Clara and peered closely at the book. It had worn down the edges and the pages had yellowed.

"I'm just guessing." Clara shrugged. "But I think I will buy it; it is only £4."

"In which case, it can't be rare. The shop owner would know the rarity of all books he gets in, it's his business to know. Trust me, I know."

"But he could have missed this one."

"Okay, I'll let you have that."

The women walked to the town centre. The German Christmas market had arrived. They passed festive chalets of heavenly smelling cookies, savoury treats, children's wooden hand-crafted toys, German sausages, and best of all, sweet crepes. Rianna and Clara ordered one each, with lashings of chocolate sauce inside. After eating, they walked under criss-crossed Christmas decorations and stopped by the enormous tree with silver baubles and twinkling lights. A sharp and crisp air blew through their coats.

"This wind is biting me! I fancy a hot chocolate and a mince pie. Let's go in here." Clara linked an arm through Rianna's and practically dragged her into a bustling, warm coffee shop.

"We just ate! And I'm not much for mince pies, but I wouldn't mind a good lemon cheesecake. I hope they sell them here," said Rianna, feeling very festive and merry.

They sat down with their beverages, Clara with a hot chocolate and a mince pie—exactly what she wanted, whereas Rianna had to settle for carrot cake with her coffee. They had run out of cheesecakes.

"How can they run out of cheesecakes? Just my luck," she grumbled.

"Cheesecakes are quite popular then, I never knew." Clara drank from her transparent mug, and then ate some of the cream from the top with a spoon.

"You definitely are not from Earth." Rianna shook her head in mock-sadness.

They ate in silence for a while, Clara on her phone and Rianna looking around her. Small children sat with their grown-ups, eating cakes and cookies, or having ice-cream. A small girl, probably aged 5 or 6, in cute powder-blue leggings and a red knitted dress waved at her. She waved back.

"She's cute, isn't she?" said Clara, putting her phone down. "I want a girl one day."

"Hmmm," said Rianna, not really listening to her. She looked like she had seen a ghost. "Oh my God." A bolt of horror went through her, and it felt like she had been punched in the gut.

"What's wrong?" asked Clara.

"It's him, Aadi. He is with someone. No, don't look at him. Hide me!"

"Too late, he is coming over."

"Oh no."

She gave Aadi a semi-smile when he approached her—with a woman. Rianna didn't recognise her. *Is she his sister?*

"Hi," said Aadi.

"This is awkward," Clara muttered under her breath but Rianna heard her. She kicked her under the table.

"Hi Aadi," said Rianna. "How are you?"

"Yeah, I am good. It's nice to see you after, well, you know. Anyway, this is Asha. Asha, this is Rianna. So, um, we are going to the market now. Bye Rianna."

"That was weird," said Rianna, watching his retreating back. "Is that his girlfriend, do you think?"

"Are you actually jealous?"

"No!" Rianna cried, and then as though convincing herself, "no, no, of course not. I'm just wondering."

"Why don't you call him tonight and find out? When was the last time you talked to him?" asked Clara.

"It was when he told me he liked me. Or was it loved me? I can't remember."

Clara gasped. "What did you just say? When did this happen, you never mentioned it! Something important like this!"

"Mention what to you?"

"That he loves you! You told me he liked you." Clara raised her eyebrows in disbelief.

"What? Look, I don't know. I'm just talking to myself. Come on, let's go home. I don't feel so good anymore. I might be coming down with something," said Rianna.

"Yeah, this thing with Aadi moving on has affected you, I can see that. Best go home and not think about it."

"It's not *affected* me." Rianna picked up her bag and stood up, making way to the door.

"Whatever you say." Clara smiled knowingly.

Rianna rolled her eyes.

Rianna lay in bed that night, wide awake. Her chest fluttered thinking of Aadi, and when she thought of him with that woman, she felt like a heavy ball was dropped into the pit of her stomach. She tossed and turned, trying to get some sleep.

Seeing Aadi had affected her, Clara was right. But she had no feelings for him. *Do I?* Why was she feeling horrible? Was she jealous, could Clara be right about that, too?

Rianna turned to her phone and went onto Facebook. She clicked onto Aadi's profile. *No, don't spy on him!* He didn't put up any personal stuff on there anyway. She put her phone back on her bedside table and sighed. Aadi was always a friend to her, why couldn't she still be happy with that?

Her phone rang, making her jump. *Aadi!* She fumbled with the phone, her nervous fingers struggling to pick it back up. She thought, for the briefest of moments, that she should just reject the call, but instead she took a deep breath and pressed accept.

"Hello Aadi," she said, feeling her heart pumping ten to a dozen.

"Hi Rianna. I just rang to explain about today." He spoke very quickly. Rianna assumed he wanted to get this conversation over and done with, or he was nervous.

"You don't have to explain. I mean you don't need to give me explanations, I didn't ask for it."

"I thought I would tell you that I met Asha by accident. We work together. But anyway, we started talking and now we are dating. It happened so fast. Rianna, I hope this is okay with you."

Rianna laughed, but it was a hollow one. "Why would I mind? I am pleased you moved on, Aadi. If we got together, it would be a disaster. We have nothing in common. I am truly happy for you. And I am sorry for not answering your calls. It was just awkward afterwards, you know, and I didn't want to let you down."

"You said you would think about it. Oh God, what have I done?" Aadi groaned.

"What are you talking about?" Rianna asked.

"You said you'd let me know in the new year. Maybe I should have waited before going out with Asha, but—"

"It's getting late…"

"It's only ten, Rianna. You can't be tired already."

"It must have been the shopping and the food. Look, Aadi. For all it's worth, I am sorry for hurting your feelings. And I am pleased you didn't wait for me and met someone else."

"I hope we can still be friends," said Aadi.

"Aadi, you are one of my best friends, and you always will be."

"Okay then, goodnight." There was a pause, then he added quickly, "Can I call you sometime next week?" he asked.

"When did you find the need to ask, silly? Of course."

"All right. Goodnight."

Rianna heard a softness in his voice. She smiled.

As she lay there going over their conversation, her eyes became as heavy as her heart, and soon she was fast asleep.

Chapter Seven

"Is it time yet? Is it, Rianna *ben*?" Jia jumped on Rianna's bed in the early hours of Christmas eve.

"Jia! It's only five. Go back to your room," Rianna said checking her phone with sleep-deprived eyes. She turned away from Jia.

"But I can't sleep! I am so excited!"

Rianna groaned as she felt her little sister bounce on her bed.

"Jia?"

"Yes." Jia kept on bouncing.

"We are not leaving until nine. Please, let me sleep. I am so tired."

"Okay, I'll let you sleep if you let me go on your drawing tablet."

The cheeky monkey! "Fine, it's on the dresser." Rianna yawned and closed her eyes again. The next thing she knew, Jia was getting into her bed. "Have you got the tablet?"

"Yes, Rianna *ben*."

"Hmmm." Rianna fell asleep straight away, knowing her sister wouldn't disturb her again. The tablet would keep her busy for some time, as it always did.

"Rianna, wake up!" Lata shouted from somewhere. "We've got to get going!"

Rianna's eyes snapped open. "What time is it?"

Lata came into her room. "It is seven. Remember, we are leaving for Windermere today, or have you forgotten? Now stop wasting time and go for your shower. I hope you have remembered to pack your bags!"

Jia skipped into the room with a lollipop in her mouth. "Papa told me wake you up. He said you must hurry. When it is 9 o'clock, he won't wait for anyone." She grinned, showing the gap in her teeth. Rianna remembered when it came out during the accident. Jia was paid £5 for that tooth. Her leg had healed well, too, so the doctor said it was okay to take off the cast after she checked it.

"Why didn't anyone wake me up earlier?" Rianna yawned.

"I did, you said it was too early," said Jia.

"It was five am, Jia. Anyway, what did you do with my tablet?"

"It's on your dresser, Rianna *ben*."

"Okay, I'm going to do Jia's hair. You hurry up now," said Lata.

Jia's natural hair was a mass of thick, dark curls that hung to her waist and couldn't be tamed, unless oil was added. Rianna's hair was medium-thick in comparison, but she chose to keep it shoulder length. Her mother disapproved, saying a girl's hair should be kept long.

Rianna planted her feet on the carpet and as she did, she remembered the night before. She was with Clara at a bar. She remembered coming home late… *was it two in the morning?* She groaned at the memory, rubbing her hand over her face. Then she saw her unpacked suitcase near the window and was glad her mother hadn't seen it.

Rianna quickly showered, dressed, and went downstairs to the kitchen. Lata washed the last pot.

"Sorry," Rianna said as she helped herself to a bowl of cereal.

"What time did you get in last night?" Lata asked in a clipped tone. She went on to pack a box with jars of spices and raw vegetables.

Rianna had a flashback of her and Jia packing a box of board games, books, and art supplies. Jia had reminded her to pack the chargers, too.

"I think around two, but I can't be too sure. I'm sorry, I shouldn't have gone out."

"Did you pack your clothes before you went out, like I said?"

"I'll do it now. It won't take me long. How long do we have?" asked Rianna.

"Just one hour. You better hurry or your papa will get mad. You know he likes to be punctual."

"What? I thought we had two hours?" Rianna ate one more spoonful of her cereal. "Can you throw the rest away? I've got to pack!" She heard her mother exclaim something angrily but didn't quite hear her as she dashed upstairs to pack that suitcase.

She wished she hadn't gone out now. She had planned to do her packing earlier that night, but then Clara rang her.

"Hey, are you busy?"

"I'm packing, why?"

"Come out with me, just for an hour. I'm dead bored. Mum has gone out with her mates and I am all alone. I promise, I won't keep you long," said Clara.

"Why can't you go out with your other friends? You know, the ones who like to drink and generally have a good time," Rianna said as she picked out a baby pink jumper, folding it neatly and placing it in her suitcase.

"I thought I would ask you first," said Clara.

"You mean they have plans too!" Rianna laughed.

"Come on, Rianna. It's Christmas Eve eve. I can't be alone tonight."

Rianna could feel her fake pouting and laughed silently, shaking her head. "Fine, okay. I'll come but only for a little while."

Of course, that 'little while' turned into a little over three hours and now she was paying for it.

"Rianna, are you ready yet?" Lata shouted from downstairs. "We are getting late, what's taking you so long?"

"I thought we had one more hour?" she shouted back.

"Actually, you only have twenty-minutes now," Jia said as she came in with another lollipop. "Have you packed the drawing tablet?"

Rianna noticed the tablet was on charge. She checked the battery; it was charged. Detaching the micro-USB from the tablet, she gave it to Jia. *Clever girl for putting it on charge.*

"You can use it in the car," she smiled at Jia.

"Can you stop, daddy? I want to go to the toilet," Jia said—again!

"This is the third time, Jia. We have already stopped twice," Rianna reprimanded her.

"Right, no more juice for you," said Lata in a decisive tone.

"One more stop then, Jia," Rajni said. "After that, no more stops. We will be leaving the motorway and entering country roads. So no more stops after this one, okay?"

"Okay," said Jia.

Jia stayed off the cartons of blackcurrant juice and fell asleep for the rest of the journey. Rianna concentrated on the route, navigating her father with the help of Google maps. Rajni could never understand the vocal instructions. Rianna looked back and saw her mother had also fallen asleep. Normally her mother would sit in the front, but her dad needed help with the instructions, which Lata was useless at.

They left the sunshine behind them as they turned into a country lane. The landscape became rolling hills and streams against a silver-grey backdrop. Rianna sighed in happiness. It was so majestic. They passed a few small waterfalls, which caught Rianna's eye. She put on her phone camera and snapped a few pictures.

"Isn't it lovely, Papa? We should make trips up north more often."

"I agree with you one hundred percent, *beta*."

It was coming up to midday now and the light was fading already. Rianna's tummy rumbled; she was famished. Unwrapping a chocolate bar, she took a bite. It felt as if someone gave her a hug.

"Do you want one, Papa?"

"No, thanks. I'll eat when we stop somewhere. Let me know when you see a café or pub around here."

They drove on for a while in silence, and then came to a small town. Rajni parked up on the road, opposite a restaurant. A small waterfall rushed down the side of the mountain opposite, the white of the water bright against the verdant green around it.

"Oh wow," she said, awestruck.

"Have we arrived?" Lata woke up, seeming dazed. She rubbed her eyes as she came around properly.

"No, we are just stopping to get something to eat. There won't be anything at the house when we arrive. I don't think I can stay hungry that long," said Rajni.

The restaurant was an inviting place, and the family welcomed the warmth coming from the fire in the hearth. The clatter of cutlery and the hubbub of chatter allowed a cheerful atmosphere. Rajni chose a corner by a big window.

"There's not much here for vegetarians, is there?" Lata screwed her face.

"There is jacket potato," Rajni pointed out. "You can have that. I'm having an all-day

breakfast. What about you girls?"

"Pizza and chips," said Jia.

"I think I will have the pasta," said Rianna.

Rajni gave the order to the waitress, and relaxed. "I like this. It's been so long since we all

have been together—just us."

Rianna relaxed too. It was going to be a very good few days with her family and no one else.

Rajni drove slowly up to the house, and Rianna gasped as she took in the scene. The house was decked in Christmas lights, and there was a real 7-foot Christmas tree to the left.

"Wow! This is amazing!" Jia exclaimed.

"Do you think Uncle is home still? We were supposed to arrive today, and not tomorrow, right?" asked Rianna.

Lata stretched. "Well, let's ring the doorbell and find out."

A man in his fifties opened the door. "Well hello! You're a bit late, I was expecting you some time ago."

"Oh, I think we are at the wrong house. We were meant to be at my brother's house, Sailesh Mehta. You don't perhaps know him; where his house is?" asked Rajni.

The man laughed. "You are in the right place. I'm Kevin. I live in the house down the road. Your brother asked me to get the fire going, you know… warm the house ready for you. And put on the lights. He is a good brother you know, not wanting you and your family to come to a cold house and all."

"Oh, well in that case, thank you, Kevin. We do appreciate it." Rajni shook Kevin's hand.

"I'd better be getting on. My wife must be wondering where I got to."

Kevin left and Rajni, along with everyone else, went into the house. It was toasty with the log burner on. The mantlepiece was decorated with tiny reindeer and sleigh sculptures, and other ornaments had been placed around the large, square living room. Original beams highlighted the high ceiling. But what Rianna love most was that the house was open plan, with a large kitchen like those you see in home and kitchen magazines. And from the kitchen, you could see the lake.

"This is amazing," Rianna felt like she was Jia's age all over again. She kneeled near the fireplace and toasted her hand. She closed her eyes, enjoying the sensation.

"Mum, look! There is a present here for all of us. Can I open mine?" Jia was sitting by the Christmas tree and shaking a large box.

"I think you can wait until tomorrow," Lata said. "Christmas Day is only a few hours away. We can open the presents after we have breakfast first thing."

"Uncle is so generous; he has thought of everything," said Rianna, amazed.

"All right, who wants to go for a stroll around the lake?" Rajni asked.

"Me, me!" Jia jumped up and down. "I'll get my wellies on!"

Rianna clutched Jia's small, gloved hand, as they walked behind their parents. The sun was shining bright now, and the air was crisp and sharp. The snow-capped mountains rose above the lake like a giant, magnificently dressed in white. Rianna lifted her face to the pale sun that gave off a slight warmth. She sighed happily and felt a freeness she hadn't experienced back home. The quietness was spectacular in its own way. It didn't break or come to a sudden halt among the peaks. She felt like she had been friends with the lake and mountains for a long time. They came to the edge of the lake and stood together watching it.

"How would you feel if we bought a holiday house out here, too?" Rajni was asking the whole family.

"Could we afford to?" Lata asked. "It would be lovely here in the summer."

"I would like it," said Rianna. "I can see us coming here often."

Rajni crouched to his smallest daughter's height. "What do you think, Jia? Would you like it here?"

"As long as I have things to do. I think staring at a lake is boring," she replied.

"I'll make sure you won't get bored."

"So, are we going to buy a house here then?" Rianna asked.

"I'll take a look at the numbers, but I think we will be able to afford one. Maybe not as big as your uncles but good enough. Right, shall we head back? My fingers are beginning to get numb."

That evening, they ate a hearty meal of pasta and salad, and then Rajni and Lata retired for the night early.

"I'm too tired from the drive," said Rajni.

"And I'm too tired from the journey," Lata said yawning. "Don't stay up too late."

Rianna and Jia settled down in front of the TV, but before long Jia was asleep on her lap. Rianna stroked her hair as she absently flicked through the channels. Her mind began to wander and she found herself thinking of Aadi, and how she felt about him. She couldn't understand why she felt like this. Wasn't he just a good friend of hers, someone she had known for years? And that girl he was with! Rianna didn't like her, not one bit. Nope, not at all!

How could Aadi find someone else so quickly when he literally just told her he liked her? *Ah, it's the green-eyed monster in you, Rianna. You are jealous he found a replacement when you bluffed his feelings for you. Shame on you.* She sighed. *But I didn't bluff his feelings, not really. I just told him to wait until I figure out how I feel about him… as a boyfriend.* Oh, that sounded weird. She had to admit she was developing some feelings for him, but it was too late to tell him that now. He had a girlfriend.

She sighed, looking at her sister. She wished she could be her age again, a time when she had no real worries. But she won't worry about Aadi anymore. She had three more days of a lovely holiday, and she was going to make the most of the peace and quiet. Rianna switched the TV off, picked up Jia, and carried her upstairs to bed.

Chapter Eight

Christmas Day

The smell of something sweet, wafted upstairs and into the bedroom where Rianna and Jia were sleeping. Rianna's nose twitched and she inhaled the aroma. Her eyes opened. *Where am I?* She squinted around the room in the semi-darkness and was able to make out the butterflies painting on the walls against a white background.

The simple white theme then followed throughout the room—from wall to furniture, carpets, and curtains. The only other colour in the room was the dusty-rose bed sheets, complete with matching pillow and duvet covers. There were two singles; Rianna slept in one and Jia in the other. This was the twin's rooms, Uncle Sailesh's daughters. The twins were from his second marriage to Urmila, after his first wife ran off with her lover and settled in New York. Luckily, he got custody of his son before she moved across the seas.

Rianna moved to the window and she was again instantly awestruck. A thick layer of fresh fluffy snow lay on the ground, and it was still snowing. Flakes petered down as if in slow motion, disappearing in a pallid lake that glittered as the sun rose, spreading light and warm colour across the land. *This* was what Rianna had been so looking forward to—the peace and tranquillity, and a Christmas with those she loved most in the world: her mum, her dad, and Jia.

"What are you looking at, Rianna *ben*?" came a small, tired voice from behind her.

"Oh, Jia. Look at this!" Rianna pulled her sister in front of her, facing the window. "What do you see?"

Jia gasped. "Ooh, it's so beautiful. Can we go and play in the snow? Please?"

Rianna laughed. "Yes, but this time we must be careful. Your leg might be healed but it's still a little weak. I'll tell you what, we can build a snowman together, okay?"

Jia nodded her head vigorously.

"Ah, there you two are. I was wondering if you would be up any time soon." Rajni was sitting in the recliner with the TV on and a newspaper in his hand. Rianna reckoned Kevin left it there for them. "We have to buy one of these chairs when we get back home. I don't know why we haven't already got one!"

The fire crackled in the hearth and the warmth enveloped Rianna in an embrace.

"I think because we already have enough furniture at home, and mum won't let you. She'll say it is a waste of money," Rianna said. "Is mum making pancakes?" She sat down on the white fluffy carpet next to the fireplace.

"I knew the smell of pancakes would wake you two up. Good morning *beta*." Lata came in singing and ever so happy. She put a plate of pancakes on the table, along with some fresh raspberries, blueberries, chopped bananas, lemon, honey, sugar, and chocolate sauce. "We needn't have brought any food with us; Urmila has stocked the fridge and cupboards for us."

Rianna, Jia, and Rajni made their way to the table. The day was perfect already. It was snowing which created a beautiful picture outside, inside it was warm and cosy, and to top it all they were enjoying fresh pancakes. It was bliss.

"Thanks Mum, and thanks to Auntie Urmila," said Rianna.

"I second that," said Rajni, and Jia giggled.

When breakfast was over, Rianna pulled her mum to one side. "Can you keep Jia busy whilst I bring the presents downstairs?"

"Go, I'll get her help me clear up in the kitchen."

Rianna kissed her mother on the cheek and went upstairs. She thought of her presents to Jia, she couldn't wait to see her face! She stole downstairs and went straight to the tree, placing the presents underneath.

"Everybody, it's present opening time!" she announced.

"Hooray!" shouted Jia and in a second, was by Rianna's side.

"Open Uncle Sailesh's present first as his was the first under the tree," said Rianna.

"It's enormous! I love it!" said Jia. It was an arts and crafts set, along with some canvas boards and acrylic paints. That should keep Jia occupied for hours.

"Now, open Mum and Dad's." Rianna pushed another large box towards Jia.

Jia opened the box to find two barbie dolls, a doll's clothes set, a house which she would have to assemble, a market, and a make-up set for the dolls.

"Thank you, thank you!" she hugged their parents.

"And now mine. This is part one. Part two will be at home, because it hasn't arrived yet," said Rianna.

"What is it?" Jia asked.

"It's a surprise. Now, open part one."

Jia's excited scream couldn't be louder. "A drawing tablet! Is this really mine?"

"Yes, and you must look after it. You are so good at drawing and as you keep on taking mine, I thought it would be best for you to have your own."

"It looks very expensive for Jia's age. She will break it," said Lata dubiously.

"It's all right mum. I have insured it and it will stay in my room when Jia is not using it. And anyway, she has not broken mine so I think it will stay safe with her," said Rianna.

"I promise to look after all my new and old stuff," said Jia. "Thank you, Rianna *ben*." She gave her a huge hug and kiss on the cheek.

Rianna got a jumper and a hard-back edition of *Sense and Sensibility*. "Where did you find this?" She flicked through the gold-leafed pages with utmost care. "I love this story."

"And you haven't got that edition either," said her father. "I knew you would love it."

Rianna laughed when she opened up the jumper. It had a picture of a stack of shelves filled with an assortment of books.

"That was your mother's idea," said Rajni.

"Thank you both. And now, you can open mine."

Lata got a new can opener—one of those that turns by itself—and a spa day, and her father got five sessions on a golf course and a flying experience. They both were happy.

"Can I play with this now?" Jia asked.

"I thought you wanted to go and play outside in the snow?" said Rianna.

"That's a good idea," said Rajni. "You two make a snowman or something, whilst your mother and I take a stroll over the bridge and around the lake again. How about it, Lata?"

"I don't like walking in the snow much," she said. "I would much prefer to stay indoors today."

"Oh, come on. It will do you good. Besides, you are always cooped up at home," said Rajni.

"Go on, Mum," said Rianna. "I'll look after Jia."

"But what about the cleaning?"

"Mum, we are on holiday. And you have already done it," Rianna pointed out.

"Okay, but you two be careful. I don't want anyone to get hurt," said Lata. "Again!"

Rianna scooped up a handful of snow and began to mound it. The snow soaked her gloves, the cold seeping into her bones. But before she could throw it, she felt something hard hit her face.

"Ow!"

Jia giggled.

"Okay, so you want to play, do you?" Rianna threw the snowball at her sister, but she missed. A laugh followed, with another snowball hitting her back this time.

"You can never beat me; I am too good!" laughed Jia.

"How's this then?" Rianna laughed as her snowball hit Jia on the leg.

Jia screamed and fell onto the snow, holding her leg. *Oh no! What have I done?*

"Oh Jia, I'm so sorry! Let me see your leg." As Rianna touched her leg, Jia laughed.

"I fooled you!"

"Jia, that was not funny. I really thought you broke your leg again!"

"Sorry Rianna *ben*. It was only a joke."

"It's okay now, but no more jokes like this please. I nearly had a heart attack! Come on, let's build this snowman."

As soon as they finished their small and wonky snowman, a bitter wind blew their way. Fierce snow particles struck Rianna and Jia, and they had to shield their eyes. The white sky turned dark and menacing.

"Let's get inside," Rianna said. "I think a snowstorm is about to hit."

As they went inside, Rianna saw her parents. Her mum didn't look so good.

"What happened?" Rianna said as she closed the door behind them.

"We weren't far, just by the bridge. Your mum slipped and landed heavily on the ice," said Rajni. "Thank God she didn't break anything."

"Ouch, my back," Lata moaned. "Help me to the sofa, the both of you."

Rianna and Rajni careful laid Lata onto the sofa.

"I'll get you a hot water bottle and some ibuprofen," said Rianna. "It's a good thing you packed those, Mum."

"Get me a blanket too," Lata said.

"Mummy, are you going to be all right?" Jia came up to Lata, holding her teddy. "I brought this for you to make you feel better." Jia gave Lata her toy.

"Oh *beta*, I am going to be alright. Thank you for your bear. But I think he will get bored with me. Why don't you and bear do some colouring together?"

"Mummy, he is just a toy. He can't do any colouring. But I think I will do some anyway."

Rianna came back with the water bottle, blanket, and the painkillers. Lata took the pills, and Rianna made her comfortable, placing the blanket over her.

"I think there is more to Mum falling over, isn't there?" Rianna said.

"Why do you say that?" asked Lata.

"I have a feeling. You are normally so careful, and you had your non-slip boots on."

"It's not fall-proof you know," said her mother.

"So, what happened?" Rianna prompted again.

"Okay, fine. I saw a black cat—it came out from nowhere. It dashed between my legs and I slipped."

"That's not really true," Rajni came into the conversation. "The cat was nowhere near you, Lata. It was walking calmly, and then you screamed. I think you scared the life out of it. Rianna, the cat jumped so high, and ran away. I was quite funny until your mother fell."

"I didn't know you were scared of cats, Mum," said Rianna.

"I'm not. But this cat was a black one, and they are bad luck when they cross your path, and this one came from nowhere. Naturally, I would be frightened. Anyway, I will be fine. Now, can you make a nice strong chai for all of us, and a hot chocolate for Jia? I'm afraid I can't do much just yet."

As Rianna got up to make the tea, she heard a series of loud beeps. Her heart sank. *So much for the peace and quiet!*

"What's that noise?" Lata said, craning her head towards the window.

"Mummy, Papa, there's a red monster truck outside!" Jia said, all excited.

Rianna went to check and when she saw who it was, her jaw clenched.

"It's Uncle Sailesh," she called over her shoulder. "What's he doing here?"

"What?" Lata and Rajni said together.

Rajni and Jia rushed to the door.

"Stay inside, Jia," said Rajni and went outside with Rianna.

"*Bhai*, what are you doing here? Shouldn't you be in New York?" Rajni addressed his older brother.

"Hello, and it is nice to see you, Rajni," Sailesh smiled, hugging his brother. "I'm sorry to barge in on your holiday. Typical British weather. All flights are cancelled until further notice."

Just great!

"So you travelled all the way here from Manchester airport? It is quite a long way," said Rajni.

"I didn't want to stay in a hotel on Christmas Day. I would rather be with family. Now, come on, help me with the bags. Ah, hello Rianna *beta*."

"Hello Uncle," said Rianna, trying to offer him a sincere smile, but secretly wishing he was anywhere but there. She went to the boot and helped grabbed the bags, as the twins, Sarika and Sanjana, and Urmila auntie stepped out of the car. When they were all inside, Rianna said she will make chai for everyone. If they were going to be invaded, at least she could hide in the kitchen. *So much for a quiet family holiday!*

Chapter Nine

Still Christmas Day

As it happened, the flight to New York was cancelled. A huge storm was blowing in from the Atlantic. Sailesh told them they stayed in a hotel the night before but decided to be with family for Christmas.

"It would be a very dull Christmas Day if we stayed in a hotel," he said with a good-natured chuckle.

For you, maybe, Rianna thought bitterly, before telling herself off for being unkind.

"Well, I am happy to see you all, *bhai*," said Rajni.

"Urmila, you did a fantastic job stocking up the house with food and drinks," Lata complimented her sister-in-law. "I wasn't sure, so I shopped before we arrived."

"You are more than welcome, *bhabhi*. But what happened, did you hurt yourself?" Urmila asked.

Urmila perched next to Lata on the edge of the sofa, her cream cashmere coat draped over her knees.

She looked like a model from a magazine, with her hair done up in a messy bun and flawless makeup. Her two daughters were the spitting image of her, although where Sarika dressed and wore make up just like her mother, Sanjana dressed plainly and wore no makeup. It was easy to tell them apart.

The others sat around the room, staring at one another in surprise. Urmila looked miserable, the twins looked miserable and bored, and Sailesh seemed strange, like there was more to this than met the eye. Lata looked at the clock, Jia huffed, and Rianna pursed her lips as she tried to think of something to say. Only Rajni seemed undisturbed.

"Kevin, your neighbour, let us in. He had the house warm and also the Christmas lights turned on outside upon our arrival. He seems like a good neighbour," said Rajni.

"Ah, Kevin. I must thank him; he is a good man, he is!" Sailesh bellowed, making everyone jump.

As if a spell was broken, everyone began talking at once, excited words pouring out in a tirade of chatter.

"I saw a black cat, Urmila," said Lata. "And I slipped on some ice. My back is quite sore."

Rianna saw her father roll his eyes and she giggled, despite her dissatisfaction at the situation.

"How terrible," said Urmila. "We must do a ritual to ward off any more evil. No wonder you fell."

"Sarika *ben*, look what Rianna *ben* got me," Jia said, showing her new the tablet.

Suddenly, Rianna remembered the chai she was meant to make. She dashed away to the kitchen, glad to be alone for a little bit. It was beginning to feel a bit like a mad Christmas Day!

When she came back with the chai, she glanced at the twins. Both girls were clever and quite with it in their own unique ways, but sometimes they acted silly and naïve. She put the tea on the table, and then went to give a cup to Lata. She then poured some tea for her uncle and her dad.

"Sarika, Sanjana, do you want some tea?" she asked.

"Yes please," they said, and came to the table.

"What have you made for me?" asked Jia.

"Hot chocolate, of course," smiled Rianna.

"Are you disappointed?" Rianna asked. "You know, about New York being cancelled?"

"Yes, and no," said Sarika. "I would miss my boyfriend for sure, but I really wanted to see New York, too. I guess it is what it is."

"Well, I am disappointed," said Sanjana. "I don't care much for boyfriends. I wanted to see the Museum of Modern Art." She sighed forlornly.

"You are so dramatic," said Sarika, rolling her eyes.

"I like museums, too," said Rianna. "Sarika, I didn't know you had a boyfriend. Aren't you a bit young?"

"What? Everyone does at our age. It's normal. Don't you have a boyfriend, Rianna *ben*?" asked Sarika.

"No… I don't."

"Yes, you do, Rianna *ben*. His name is Aadi!" Jia shouted.

The room went deathly quiet, and everyone turned to stare at Rianna.

Oh, just great!

"Aadi? Who is Aadi?" Urmila asked, seeming delighted to have a new and tantalising subject to discuss. "Is he a boyfriend or a fiancée?"

"I wish," said Lata. "He is just a friend—or so she insists. I keep telling her to find someone to marry. She is twenty-seven, far too old to remain single in my opinion."

"Mum, I'm twenty-five, not twenty-seven!" Rianna said crossly. She crossed her arms around her chest. "And now people are getting married after the age of thirty."

"*Hai Ram*! Is that true?"

"Yes, *Kaki*," said Sarika and Sanjana together.

"Look everyone, it's Christmas Day. Let's start making Christmas dinner, shall we? Let's make this like a party!" Sailesh's eyes met Rianna's, and he gave her a sympathetic nod.

"Thank you," Rianna mouthed, grateful that his presence was good for one thing, at least.

"That is a good idea," said Lata forgetting about the subject of Rianna and marriage. "Urmila, you take lead. I'll help you." Lata tried to get up but shouted in pain.

"Better still, I will make the dinner with Rianna, and the twins can help. You are in no state to get up," said Urmila.

"If you say so," said Lata feigning disappointment, but Rianna saw the glint in her mother's eye.

As the dinner was under way, the men opened a bottle of whisky and relaxed. Rianna heard the TV being switched on.

"Christmas Day will not be uneventful this year," said the weather girl. *You're telling me!* "A ferocious snowstorm is coming in from the Atlantic and will cause severe travel disruptions. Be safe and travel only if necessary. Also…"

Sailesh switched the channel to a Christmas movie. "Do you think the storm will last?" he asked.

"No, it's England. Nothing lasts here. It's all hype. But you have two weeks off, don't you? You can fly off as soon as the weather clears," said Rajni taking a gulp of his whisky.

"Yes, but I have missed today, the best part of the trip. That was whole point of going to New York—to experience Christmas over there. But never mind, I'll make it up to the girls next year."

"They are good kids, they'll understand. They are now, what? Sixteen?" asked Rajni.

"Sixteen and growing up really quickly. Look at our Rianna and Jia. I'm glad Rianna isn't marrying too early. Let her travel and enjoy her life," said Sailesh.

"I agree. Anyway, she is busy with the shop and she likes it. I'll leave it up to her when she decides to marry. I am in no hurry, unlike Lata. Besides, I am selfish. I don't want to lose her. I will miss her too much."

"Oh Papa." Rianna came over and sat on the arm of the sofa, putting an arm over Rajni's shoulders. "I won't be marrying anytime soon. I'm afraid you are stuck with me for a long time yet, and remember you have Jia, too. We won't let you off daddy duties yet."

All three laughed.

"I like your attitude, *beta*," said Sailesh.

They looked towards Jia who was playing Jenga with the twins. Jia was focussed intently on the pieces and seemed determined to win. Rianna supposed that if they couldn't have the quiet Christmas they hoped for, at least Jia was having fun.

Suddenly, a loud and long beep broke their attention, and everyone was fixed towards the window. *What now!* Rianna went out to see. The storm had arrived, and she had to strain to see who it was in the midst of two strong headlights glaring her way.

Through fast falling snow, Rianna made her way to the car.

"Rianna, be careful!" said Rajni from the doorway. "Wait, I'll come too!"

"It's okay!" Rianna shouted above the noise from the car. "Stay where you are."

She reached the car, and gasped.

"Clara! What are you doing here? What's wrong?" Rianna shouted over the howling wind and Mariah Carey's voice bellowed from the stereo. "Can you shut that off!"

"What? I can't hear you!" shouted Clara.

Rianna pointed at the stereo system. "Shut that thing off!"

"What?"

Rianna groaned. She wriggled her body through the open window and shut the music off. She wriggled out again.

"Oh, that's what you were saying," Clara laughed. "Move away then so I can open the door."

"What are you doing here anyway?" Rianna asked as they began to trudge back to the house.

"You asked me to come, remember?"

"No, I don't remember. When did I ask you?" Rianna shivered in the cold, but inside her irritation burned. This situation was impossible! She loved these people, but she had wanted a couple of days away from them and they had followed her!

Then she heard a faint meow.

"Is that...?" she began to ask but stopped. It was probably the wind.

"What?"

"Nothing. Let's get inside. It's freezing." But then she heard it again. "Clara, do you have a cat in the car?"

"Oh I forgot about Bunny!"

"Bunny?"

"The kitten!" Clara rushed back to the car and came back with a small bundle in a blanket. It meowed.

"Let's get inside, I don't want Bunny to freeze. Poor darling!"

They closed the door behind them, and peace and quiet reigned... for all of two seconds.

"Who is this?" asked Urmila.

"Clara! What a surprise!" Lata exclaimed.

"Clara *ben*, what are you holding?" asked Jia.

"Hello everyone," said Clara. She threw everyone a nervous smile, then spoke to Rianna from the corner of her mouth. "I didn't realise you were having a party."

"No, neither did it," Rianna muttered.

"Clara is my friend, and she works for me at the shop, too," she said to the others.

The kitten meowed. Clara sat down next to the fire and revealed a tiny tabby.

"This is Bunny," said Clara. The tabby stood up and drew nearer to the heat, yawning and stretching.

There was a collective *aww*. The kitten meowed what seemed like a *hello*.

"Can I pick her up?" Jia asked.

"Why not? She is yours," said Clara. "It's a present from your sister but remember, she is not just for Christmas but for life."

"Oh, no no. I am having no pet in my house. I don't want a cat bringing in dead animals. You take it back, Clara," said Lata.

"No Mummy, I want to keep it," said Jia. "I'll be good. I'll take care of her forever. She can sleep in my room."

"Relax, Mrs Mehta. This is a house cat. It doesn't go out at all. House cats like their creature comforts," said Clara.

"But what about the pet hairs? Is it house trained? The cost of the food, vet bills…"

"Don't worry, Mum. Jia and I will look after all of that," said Rianna.

Lata looked at her husband. "Well, don't you have anything to say?"

"I am happy for the kids if they are happy," he said merrily.

"You have had too much to drink!" said Lata.

"I can't believe you came all the way here to deliver the cat in this weather," said Rianna.

"Well, you did invite me, too. What else would I do on Christmas Day?"

"Right," Rianna said with a resigned sigh. "Let's get your stuff out of the car. You brought a bag with you I hope?"

Clara nodded.

"Good, then we can talk in private!"

"Did I really invite you? Why can't I remember that?"

"Because you were drunk. But now I hope you really do want me here," said Clara.

"I want you here more than anything," Rianna reassured her, even if it wasn't quite the truth. They stood inside the snug, double-glazed balcony patio, holding steaming mugs of hot chocolate topped with whipped cream and marshmallows, and they looked over the lake as they talked. "And thank you for bringing Bunny for Jia, I appreciate it."

"She was no problem. I wanted to keep her at one point. I may get myself one after New Year's." There was a hint of a sad tone in Clara's voice.

"Is everything okay, Clara? There seems to be something odd about you today. And, you know, you've driven all this way."

"It's nothing." She raised her cup to her lips, hiding her expression behind the bounds of whipped cream.

"I am your best friend, you know. You can't keep things from me. Now, spill."

"You promise to not tell anyone?"

"I promise."

Clara took a deep breath. "I think I may be pregnant with Michael's baby." Clara said it so fast Rianna wasn't sure she heard right.

"Did you just say you are pregnant?"

"Don't say it too loud, someone might hear!"

"We are at the back, no one will be able to hear us. But Clara, this is big! Does Michael know? Does you mum know?"

"No and no. I don't know myself really. I have missed my period. It's been two weeks and I feel nauseous most days. I am scared to do a pregnancy test. I came here to try and get my mind off it."

"All the shops are closed today, of course. We can get a test tomorrow morning at the local pharmacy," said Rianna sympathetically.

"Actually Rianna, I have a test with me. I have been carrying it around with me for a week," Clara said in a timid tone.

"Well, what are you waiting for? Do the test now and get it over with. At least then you know if it is positive or negative. And whatever happens, I will support you all the way."

Clara took a deep breath. "I was hoping you would say that. Okay, let's do it."

"Clara, how long are you going to take?" Rianna knocked on the door.

"I'm done, I'll come out in a minute!"

Rianna felt so nervous, she couldn't even imagine how Clara must be feeling. Having a baby and bringing it up was a huge thing, and she had a feeling Clara would not be ready for such a responsibility. Then there was the question of getting support from her mum and Michael. How would they react?

She heard a flush, and the taps going. Then, Clara opened the door.

"Well?"

"I am pregnant," she said, and then suddenly began to cry. "I don't know what to do. Mum and I had an argument as well."

"About what?"

"She wants me to move out of the house," Clara said between gulps. "I can't afford that and now with the baby… oh Rianna! I don't know what to do!"

"Why does she want you to move out?"

"She wants her boyfriend to move in with her. She said I am old enough to get my own place. And she tells me this on Christmas Day!"

"Okay, look, take a deep breath and calm down. We will figure this out. Talk to Michael first. Then you will call your mum and tell her. She will understand."

"I really hope so. I don't want to be homeless with a baby in tow."

"Worst case scenario, you can stay upstairs in the bookshop until well, let's just see. And it is Christmas. Why don't we enjoy the rest of the day? When you are back home, you can tell Michael. He is a good guy; he will support you all the way. And once your mum knows too, there will be no chance of her kicking you out. She'll be delighted to have a grandchild."

"I wish I had your confidence."

Rianna gave her a huge smile and a hug. "Now, put some make-up back on your face. We don't want that lot down there see your blotchy face. Especially my mum and auntie, they are nosey so and so's! Go into that room—I have my make-up bag on the dressing table."

As Clara went off, Rianna's phone rang. It was a WhatsApp video call from Damini!

Chapter Ten

"Oh, you look beautiful," said Rianna as she looked down at the screen. "And what a lovely surprise. Are you married already?"

Rianna wasn't exactly close to her cousin, Damini, her *maasi's* daughter in India, so she was genuinely surprised to receive a video call from her—and on her wedding day, especially. She was dressed in her bridal *lehenga* with make-up that enhanced her natural grey eyes and her already flawless complexion.

"Rianna *ben*, I need your help. You are the only one who can do it! Make Ma understand." Rianna detected desperation in her voice. *Oh no.*

"What's going on, Damini, is everything alright?"

"I can't… I can't get married to Nilesh. I just can't do it!"

"Okay. Calm down and breathe, and then begin slowly," Rianna advised.

"Okay," said Damini, now tearful.

Just then, the bathroom door opened, and Clara came out.

"Sorry, I didn't know you were on the phone," she said as she saw the look of panic in Rianna's face. "I'll be downstairs," she mouthed.

"Thanks Clara, I won't be long."

As Clara went downstairs—she looked to be in a better mood—Rianna went back to Damini.

"If you are busy, I can go away," Damini volunteered. "Are you having a party? You know, as it is Christmas?"

An unwanted one, maybe.

"No, I am not busy. Now tell me what all this is about." Rianna went into the twins' room and sat cross-legged on the bed.

"It's well, embarrassing," Damini began. "We met on Shaadi.com and we liked each other straight away. We visited each other a few times and got to know each other. The families met and before we knew it, we were engaged. Then just last night he told me he…"

"Rianna saw her face had gone red. "And what happened?"

"He said he can't have children anymore because he had a vasectomy."

"What?" Rianna shouted. She covered her mouth. "What did you say?" she whispered, hoping no one heard her shout.

"He is divorced. His ex-wife made him. She didn't want any more children."

"Why didn't he tell you all this before?"

"I don't know. I suppose he was scared. He still wants to marry me, and I thought I wanted to as well. Now, I am unsure. He is a good man, Rianna."

"But Damini, this is huge! Does he have any children?"

"He has a five-year-old daughter. She is sweet; she and I have fallen in love with one another. She has started to call me Mummy. Her own mother has given full custody to Nilesh and has decided to move to Singapore to concentrate on her career."

"Rianna, where are you?" Rianna heard her mother's voice.

"It's Mum. Hang on… don't go away." Rianna left the phone on the bed, tiptoed to the door, and craned her neck around it. Lata was outside, along with Urmila and the twins.

"I'm on the phone, Mum. Can this wait?"

"To whom? Is it Aadi?" Lata asked.

"What? No! Why are you so obsessed by him?"

"I'm not."

"Yes, you are".

"Okay, calm down and listen. Your *maasi*, Damini's mum, called. She is frantic with worry. She can't find Damini anywhere. If she calls you—"

"Isn't Damini getting married today? And why would she call me? We are hardly close cousins." Rianna hoped they believed her.

"I don't know all that. But that's a good question. Anyway, your *maasi* said if you do receive a call from her, we must let her know immediately. That Damini, I don't know what she is doing, going missing at such a time. Do you know the *marajh* has called for her come to the mandap four times already. Everybody is ready for her; God knows what her in-laws would think about us!"

"Mum, we are not there and there is no 'us' in their wedding."

"But we are from the girl's side, so this looks bad on us too." Lata looked at Rianna suspiciously. "This is important, Rianna. Your *maasi* is going mad with worry, my poor sister. Rianna, you make sure you don't do this to me on your wedding day. May He have mercy on me!"

"Mum, stop being a drama queen."

The twins sniggered.

"Look, I have to go back on the call. I'll be down in a bit," Rianna said before her mother could say anything more. "If I get a call from Damini, I'll let you know, okay?"

Lata gave Rianna a look of resignation mixed with a 'you'd better.' Then Rianna noticed something.

"Your back, it seems to be better. You are no longer in pain, are you?"

"It is much better. It must be one of those temporary things," Lata said dismissively, although she blushed. "Let's go downstairs, Urmila, girls. Let's leave Rianna to her phone call with Aadi."

"I'm not talking to Aadi." Rianna wanted to scream, but she remained calm.

"Whatever you say," Lata chuckled and went downstairs.

Rianna groaned and went back to Damini.

"Sorry for being gone for so long." Rianna told her cousin about the conversation she just had with her mother. "You've got to speak to *maasi*."

"That's why I called you, I don't know how to. I can't talk to anyone else here; it's too embarrassing. And I knew you would be able to help."

"Can I ask a question?"

"Yes."

"Do you think you want to marry him? Look at it like this, would you be happy to be a mum to his daughter, knowing you can't have any of your own. Unless his operation is reversed—it can happen, you know. Does your mum know about his daughter?"

The look on Damini's face said it all.

"Oh dear. Well, where are you now?"

"I'm hiding in my room at the hotel—this is where the wedding is taking place. Ma came in to find me, but I hid in a cupboard."

"You want me to talk to *maasi*, don't you? What do you want me to say?"

"I want you to talk to your mum and ask her to talk to mine. They are sisters, they will be able to discuss this with no embarrassment. I can't do this alone."

"Leave it with me and stay where you are. I'm sending your mother to you. Don't worry, it will all be fine. Just one thing, do you love this man?"

"I do."

"That's where we will start then."

"Yes, that's right. Just talk to her calmly," Lata advised her sister.

"How could she keep something like this? We used to be friends, not like mother or daughter. Damini used to tell me everything!"

Rianna sat by Lata's side, and looked at her crying *maasi* on the phone screen. She was glad she was able to tell her mother everything in private, away from Urmila and the girls. Poor *maasi* and Damini.

"Stop crying, Lila," Lata said to her older sister. "Dry your eyes and go and speak to Damini, but you might want to stall the wedding a little longer. If you want my advice, call the wedding off for the time being. How can Damini marry a man who has had an operation of—you know. And he has a daughter too. Damini is 28."

"Mum, she is thirty-five," said Rianna.

"Really? I didn't know that. Sorry, Lila. Even so, it doesn't mean Damini has to settle for anything less. Now, go and speak to her, then ring me back. I want to know what her decision is." Lata ended the call. "Well, that is that."

Rianna put her head on her mother's shoulder. "I'd hate to be in such a position. I just hope Damini can make a decision that is right for her."

"Me too," said Lata and planted a kiss on her daughter's forehead. "Let's go downstairs. I bet Urmila has a glass to the ceiling, trying to hear our conversation."

The two burst out in laughter.

It was coming up to three o' clock, and the storm was getting worse.

"Ah, there you two are," said Rajni. "Did you talk to your sister, then?"

"Yes, it is all fine now," Lata replied. Rianna was there when her mum told her dad that her *maasi* called, and nothing else. She was sure her mother would fill in the details later when they were alone.

"Good, good. When is dinner ready? I am a starving man." Rajni stretched and got up from his seat. He went to the window. "I think I will go for a walk outside. Do you want to come, *bhai*?"

"The storm is getting worse, Mr. Mehta," said Clara. "I don't think it is a good idea."

"Nonsense, it is only a bit of snow!" Rajni laughed. As he turned away from the window, Sailesh got up from his chair.

"It's not a bad idea."

As the men prepared to go outside, the doorbell rang. Rianna's gut twisted as she opened the door. *How many more people can turn up?*

"Surprise!"

"Meenakshi *maasi*!" Rianna exclaimed.

Chapter Eleven

Boxing Day

Meenakshi came bustling into the house, with Peter, Jay, and Anaya in tow. She was laden with bags of wrapped presents.

Rianna rolled her eyes as she held the door open for them. *More visitors!*

"Hello everyone," Meenakshi cried as she dumped the bags on the living room floor and looked around at the crowd. "Oh, it's a full house! Lata, I didn't know you were having a party."

Lata hugged her sister. Rianna could see her mother's delight at having all these guests, but her own stomach churned with irritation.

"Why are you here?" Lata asked, holding her sister out at arms' length as though to get a better look. "Are you mad? Travelling in this storm!"

"We left before the storm hit but Jay wanted to stop at various points to take pictures on his new camera. It was a Christmas present from Peter. By the time we were nearing Windermere, the storm hit. It's not that bad really, my car did its job perfectly. It didn't skid and it was a smooth ride."

"Speak for yourself," said Anaya. "I swear Mum was going to kill us around those hair-raising bends! I warned her too about the storm."

Peter shook hands with Rajni and Sailesh and settled down on a chair.

"I think some whisky is in order, then," said Rajni, pouring his brother-in-law a glass.

"After that hell ride, I think so!" Peter said.

"I have two big softies in my family. What happened to your 'nerves of steel', eh?" Meenakshi demanded. "At least my Jay is courageous. He is never scared of anything, isn't that right, *Bittu*?"

"*Bittu*!" laughed Sarika. "What a name!"

"It's a nickname," said Jay, his face colouring. "Mum, how many times have I told you not to call me that. My name is Jay, the real name you and Papa gave me."

"But it was your *dadi-ma* who gave that name to you. I think *Bittu* is a lovely name," Meenakshi said.

"What is your nickname, Mum?" Anaya asked, smiling manically.

"What has that got to do with anything?"

"Jay, her mum named her *Jalebi*, did you know that?"

"I love jalebis," said Peter. "I could eat them all day long."

"Coming to Mum's nickname, maybe you should call her *Jalebi*, Dad," said Jay.

"I don't think so!" said Meenakshi. "That is a horrible name. What was my mother thinking?"

"I rest my case! So, no more *Bittu*, okay, Mum?" said Jay.

Rianna watched her family from the corner of the room. All she wanted was a peaceful Christmas, now it was a madhouse full of weird family characters. She tried to smile, but it was at best.

Her gaze moved to Jia and the kitten. Jia was watching a Christmas cartoon, stroking Bunny's ears will the cat slept on her little lap. The fire burned on merrily.

Rianna's mind wandered to Damini. Did she get married to that man? If it were her in that position, would she marry a man who had a child and couldn't have any more? No, she didn't think she would.

Besides, marriage was very far from her mind. She wanted to concentrate on her bookstore, and maybe someday she would also write a book. She had no idea what on though, maybe she could write fiction. It shouldn't be too hard. She could join an evening class at the college and study a Creative Writing course. She also wanted to travel and enjoy what life had to offer. Marriage was not in her vision in the immediate future, so her mum would have to forget about it at least for now.

"So, shall we have some Christmas dinner now?" said Lata. "Urmila, do we have enough?"

There would have been enough if we hadn't been invaded!

"Oh, don't you worry, I bought some food for us from home. Good Indian food—*theplas*, potato curry, very hot fried chilli, and a box of sweets and chocolates," said Meenakshi.

"Now, that's what I like to hear. Good old chillies!" Urmila said.

"None for me," said Jay and Anaya together.

"Or us," the twins said. "Give me a pizza any day!"

"We are having a roast chicken and all the trimmings, I hope. I don't want Indian food today, thanks. It is Christmas, so Christmas food it has to be," Rajni said this with a finality.

"Actually, Dad. The traditional Christmas bird is a turkey, not chicken," said Rianna.

"I don't like turkey, I find it a bit too dry," said Peter. "My mum was very traditional, every year we had to have turkey. There were no substitutes."

"Lucky for you, we have two. Chickens, that is, not turkeys. I bought one from home, and Urmila also bought one. We have enough veggies too, so enough for us all," Lata exclaimed triumphantly as if she had made a new discovery.

"Let's have some Christmas music!" Sailesh bellowed.

"Hear, hear!" Peter said.

Then, to everyone's astonishment and Jia's giggles, the men stood up and began to dance. Meenakshi and Urmila joined in, and then Rianna gasped when her mother joined in too. Laughter rang out through the room, and everywhere she looked, Rianna saw wide grins and sparkly eyes. She gritted her teeth, wishing once again for that peaceful Christmas she'd dreamt of, but even she had to admit the atmosphere was a jolly one.

Anaya and Jay leapt up next, and Rianna raised her eyebrows in surprise, her lips twitching into a smile. It was when the twins grabbed her arm, though, that she gave in, laughing freely as they dragged her to her feet. Jia put the kitten down and began jumping around the room. And everybody danced, ate, drank, and danced again.

Eventually, Rianna sat back, her laughter dying and being replaced by a gentle, satisfied smile. Everyone was so happy—including her, to her surprise—and everything really was perfect.

Maybe having a mad Christmas isn't really mad at all.

Rianna tiptoed downstairs in the absolute quiet, but her head was pounding. Did she drink too much? Her memory was hazy, but she got flashes of Clara telling her to drink for her and her mother asking Clara if she was pregnant.

"What! No, of course not Mrs. Mehta. It's just that I have decided to give the drink up, for my health." Clara could never lie to save her life.

"If you say so," said Lata, a look of 'I know when I know' on her face. And at that point, Rianna began to laugh. Yes, she was very drunk at that time. She groaned at the thought of it.

She made herself a strong black coffee and sat watching the lake. The sun shone full force, glittering over the calm waters of the lake, and Rianna squinted at the brightness. The storm had gone and had left clear, crisp, blue skies. She sighed. If only she and her family were left alone, then she wouldn't be feeling so weary. She had enjoyed the dancing and singing, but it hadn't quite been the Christmas she was hoping for.

She walked over to the lounge area and watched her cousins and Jia strewn over the floor, gentle snores coming from somewhere in the middle. Once the impromptu party had finished, the women had got together to discuss the sleeping arrangements.

"Clara, you can sleep in the twins' room with Rianna," said Urmila. "Jia will sleep in the living room with the twins and Anaya. And Jay can have the spare room at the back."

"Can I have Bunny with me?" Jia asked.

"Of course you can," said Rajni, smiling widely. "What a fabulous day this has been!"

"Why do I have to sleep in the back?" Jay moaned. "It's cold there."

"Don't worry, we have put the central heating on. It will warm up in no time," said Meenakshi. "Now, stop being grumpy. It's the least Urmila *ben* could do after we invited ourselves!"

"I am glad you all came," said Urmila. "You all are always welcome."

All the couples had a room to themselves and despite the amount of guests, the sleeping arrangement worked out well.

I need my sunglasses. Rianna made her way back upstairs. Clara was snoring away, and so she tiptoed to her bag, rummaging through it to find them. *Ah, here they are!* She put them on and things began to look much better, her head pounding a little less.

She noticed it was deathly silent if you discounted the snores. There were no police or ambulance sirens, no traffic noise, and no voices. Just the quiet. Maybe she should lie down for a second, just for a bit…

"Rianna *ben*! Wake up!" Rianna found Jia bouncing on her bed. She groaned.

"Go away," she moaned. "You are making me feel sick."

Jia stopped jumping and climbed off the bed. "Are you okay, Rianna *ben*? You don't look so good."

"That's because she is Miss Grumpy this morning," said Clara. "You go downstairs, I'll wake her up."

Rianna squinted and her friend's face swim before her. She groaned again, burying her head in her hands.

"I told you not to drink so much," Clara said, grinning.

"No, if I recall, you said I should drink on your behalf," Rianna croaked. Her throat burned.

"Yes, but you didn't have to drink like a fish. Anyway, get up and make yourself presentable. It is eleven, and some of your family, and I are leaving soon."

"What? Why are you going? Please don't go, I will miss you," said Rianna, slowly getting up and realising how true that was. She hadn't wanted all these guests, but now they were there, she didn't want them to leave.

"I think you are still drunk," Clara laughed.

They all sat in the lounge after breakfast, chatting amiably. Everyone was happy, apart from her, it seemed. Rianna could almost hear her dad mocking her, "You should learn to control your drink, Rianna *beta*. Look at your mother; she is a good example."

She would reply back, "That's because she doesn't drink, Papa."

Rianna smiled despite herself, looking around at her wonderful, crazy, loving family. She was glad they had a good time and grudgingly, she had to admit that she had enjoyed it, too. She knew how lucky she was to have such a family, and she was grateful they had all turned up—albeit uninvited— and made Christmas special. She *had* wanted a quiet Christmas, but them being there hadn't been so bad, after all. It was a blessing in disguise, and a Christmas she would remember forever.

"What time is your flight, *bhai*?" asked Rajni.

"In three hours' time. We will be making a move soon. But I want you to stay here for as long as you like. There is no hurry to rush back to Leicester, is there?" Sailesh said.

"It all depends on Rianna. Lata doesn't work as you know, Jia is on her school holidays, and I don't go back to work until 2nd January," Rajni replied.

"We can stay a little longer if you want, Dad," said Rianna.

Beep Beep!

"Who could that be?" asked Lata, looking around the room. "Everybody is here already!"

Urmila went to open the door, then glanced back with both intrigue and excitement. "There is someone here with a bouquet of red roses, and a very large one! Is anyone expecting flowers?"

"No," came a chorus of voices. Rianna's heart began to race. *It couldn't be… could it? No, of course not. It can't be… but could it?* She felt silly but she wanted to know anyway.

She rose slowly from her chair, and she went to the door to investigate.

It felt as though time had slowed and when she saw him standing there, she swallowed. The rest of the world melted away and suddenly, it was only the two of them: Rianna in the doorway and Aadi— handsome, funny Aadi—with the biggest, most beautiful bunch of roses Rianna had ever seen.

"Aadi! What are you doing here?"

"Hello," said Aadi, shifting nervously. "I thought I would surprise you."

"It's certainly a surprise," she said, unsure what else to say. But her heart was beating very fast, and her palms felt clammy. *Why am I sweating? It's -1 out here!*

"So, this is the Aadi everyone is talking about," Meenakshi cooed, peering over Rianna's shoulder. "Come in, come in—we all want to meet you! Rianna, don't keep him standing outside. It's freezing!"

"But… he is not invited!" Rianna stammered. *What was going on?*

"Thank you. Um… this is for you, Rianna." Aadi gave the roses to her and smiled awkwardly, half-expecting to be shot down for the romantic gesture. She took them to a chorus of awws from her family.

"Er, thanks." Rianna took the flowers, unsure how she felt. She hadn't wanted him there, but then… then he was stood in front of her and she realised that yes, yes this was what she had wanted all along. Seeing him was what she had wanted.

Aadi, with a huge grin on his face, stepped inside. Lata, Urmila, and Meenakshi ushered him into the lounge, chatting rapidly and guiding him to a chair. Rianna was left standing with the flowers, suddenly feeling inadequate and overwhelmed. She took a deep breath and followed.

"It's so nice of you to come all the way here, it is a lovely surprise. I am sure Rianna appreciates it," said Lata, shooting her daughter a warning look—*don't mess this up, Rianna.* "Don't you, *beta*?"

"Yes, it is a nice gesture. Do you think, um, I can talk to him in private? Aadi, fancy a walk?"

"How romantic!" Urmila gushed; her hands clasped in front of her chest. "A walk in the snow."

"You never take me for a walk in the snow," Meenakshi said, playfully slapping Peter on the arm.

Jay made a gagging gesture and Anaya laughed out loud, but the twins seemed to be already infatuated by Aadi.

"Aadi *bhai*, do you like Bunny? She is my cat. Clara *ben* brought it here for me," said Jia.

"She is cute," said Aadi, tickling the cat's forehead. It purred.

Great, even the bloody cat likes him!

"Well, Aadi?" Rianna asked, tickled by an annoyance she didn't understand—and by something else, a feeling of... *what?*

"Yes, sorry. Thank you everyone," Aadi said.

As they stepped outside, Rianna saw her family huddled at the window, staring at them. She rolled her eyes, took a deep breath, and did her best to ignore them.

"I am surprised you came," said Rianna. "And on Boxing Day. Shouldn't you be with your girlfriend?"

"She isn't my girlfriend. We split up." They walked along the side of the glittering lake. "It is so beautiful here, don't you think, Rianna?"

"Why did you split up with her?"

"With whom?"

"With her, the one you were with at the coffee shop."

"Oh her. We weren't really together. I mean, we were, but not really, if you get what I mean," said Aadi.

"I don't," said Rianna in a dull tone. "Please, explain. I am intrigued."

"Oh, you're being sarcastic."

"No, I'm not. I am really interested. I mean, she was really into you and vice versa, so what happened for you to break up?"

"Look, I realised she wasn't the one for me. I was never *really into her*. She was just... a substitute for something I really wanted. *Someone* I really wanted." He stopped walking and turned to her, looking deep into her eyes, and she held her breath. "It is you, Rianna; it has always been you."

They were on the bridge, the lake flowing beneath them, and around them perfect white snow. It was beautiful and serene and yet, the only thing Rianna could focus on was Aadi. She didn't know this version of him, the one who seemed so in love with her. She had known a whimsical Aadi, funny Aadi, carefree Aadi. She knew the Aadi who didn't care in relationships, only having casual, shallow flings— never serious.

"What do you say? Shall we give it a go?" Aadi asked.

"Aadi, I want to, I really do." She pressed her lips together and looked away from him, her eyes settling on the distant hills.

"But you don't want to get in a relationship with me?"

"No, it's not that." She turned back to him with a sigh. "To be honest, I was annoyed and jealous when I saw you with that girl—and I wouldn't even admit it to myself. Not at first. Don't laugh, but this feeling is new to me. I don't think I have ever felt this."

"What, are you saying you have never been out with anyone?" He creased his brow, lost in thought.

"Actually, I don't recall you going out with a man."
He gasped and grinned. "Are you gay?"

"Aadi!" Rianna pushed him playfully, perhaps a
little too much, and he fell onto the snow. "Oops,
sorry," she said, wide-eyed but with laughter on her
lips, too. He used the railings of the bridge to pull
himself up, his eyes sparkling with amusement.

"It's okay." He dusted the snow off his jeans and
grinned up at her. "So, you were saying you were
jealous."

"And annoyed," Rianna reminded him, her tone
firm. "The thing is, I do have some feeling for you,
and we can go out. But if you are talking about
marriage, think again!"

"Who said anything about getting married? We can
take our time," he said.

"Really?" Her heart fluttered in her chest. *He
understands me!*

"Really. Let's take it one day at a time."

When they arrived back at the house, he stopped
and took her hand.

"Aadi!" she said alarmed. "You said—"

"Rianna Mehta," he interrupted, staring deep into her eyes, making her stop. "Would you do me the honour of going out with me?" He took out a plastic box and opened it, then threw her one of his silly, happy grins.

She fell back laughing, her hand still in his, and she nodded. "Yes, Aadi. Yes, I will."

Inside the box, an edible sweet ring glinted in its cellophane wrapper.

"You had me worried for a minute there," she said.

He looked up at her and winked, then undid the cellophane and put the sweet on her finger.

They jumped as they heard a humongous, roaring cheer from the house.

Oh, just great!

The End

About the Author

Malika J Gandhi is a multi-genre author. She writes YA Fantasy, romance, historical, Paranormal mysteries.

She lives with her husband and two sons in the East Midlands, UK. She is a homemaker and in between caring for her family, she writes her books and dabbles in art. She is keen on movies, art galleries and history museums and is curious about the universe.

More Titles

Love in the Time of the Monsoon

Where the Secret Lies

Aanchal

Buy on Amazon

https://amzn.to/3oJjdFT

Printed in Great Britain
by Amazon